Acclaim for Jernigan Pontiac and *Hackie: Cab Driving and Life*

"Burlington and environs are to Pontiac like a special and loving, if eccentric, relative. He warmly observes human nature as much as he watches the road. Usually, he likes what he sees, and judging from *Hackie*, there's hope in this crazy world."

— *The Burlington Free Press*

"Pontiac has the emotional acuity and linguistic flair to present us with such intimate portraits of people that our interest in 'the old verities and truths of the heart,' as Faulkner called them, is renewed with each story in his book. . . . But what makes his stories so insightful is that Pontiac displays the non-judgmental magnanimity we might come to expect of a wise judge or monk."

— *The County Courier*

"What an amazing writer. He offers a fun, first-person perspective into things we can only wonder about."

— *From the New England Press Association First-Place Award*

ALSO BY JERNIGAN PONTIAC

Hackie: Cab Driving and Life

June 2006

Dear Mary Frances:

HACKIE 2

PERFECT AUTUMN

BY JERNIGAN PONTIAC

Thanks for being a Hackie fan!

Jernigan Pontiac

These are revised versions of stories first published in the newspapers,
The Vermont Times and *Seven Days*.

ISBN 0-9753056-1-1
First Printing May 2006

Thanks to: Donald Eggert for cover design and typesetting;
Seven Days for the newspaper's support in production and marketing;
Glenn Russell and the Burlington Free Press for the cover photo;
and Sarah Ryan for the Hackie illustration.

For additional copies of Hackie books contact the official *Hackie* website:
www.yohackie.com

Printed in the U.S.A. by
Morris Publishing
3212 East Highway 30
Kearney, NE 68847
1-800-650-7888

Dedicated to Ruth Christine Solomon –
my brave companion of the road

ACKNOWLEDGEMENTS

Heartfelt thanks to all the folks who continue to fool me into believing I have something worthwhile to say. Without the support of my friends, family and loyal readers, I don't think I could write these stories. I just wouldn't have the heart. I'm so very grateful for your encouragement and love.

To the heart of my heart, Moreno and Teresa Robbins; the unbelievably gracious Jesse Solomon; Prabhupada dasa; every single one of those Bocks, especially my big sister Melly; Jane Johnson, my biggest supporter; Doris and Arthur Robbins; Sunny Barker and the Barker boys; Wendy and Alex Rossell; Steve and Judy Robbins.

All four of the Webbs, each one more beautiful than the next; Eric Perkins and Dianne Deptula, especially for the spiritual camaraderie which I need like air; all the Us', especially Stefani Ji.

Thanks to my amazing editors, Pamela Polston, Paula Routly and Ruth Horowitz, who, week after week, make me look like a much better writer; Shay Totten, who first believed in me and gave me a shot; Rick Woods, Don Eggert, Peter Freyne and the entire splendid staff at *Seven Days*; and Rick Kisonak, who somehow knew I could be a writer even before I did.

Michael Jewel; Ray Victory; Jim Finch; Matt Kelsh; Mike Ohler; Todd and Susan Comen; Nort Wyner; Eric and Gladys Zelman; Kristin D'Agostino (my savvy cat); Rich and Delane Moser; Ted and Winnie Looby (thanks for letting me play in the band); Paul Gale and Meg Beliveau; Ed and Betty Levin; Matty Beliveau; Tom Thurber; Robert Rosenthal; Jerry Michaels; David and Sally Conrad, two peace-loving people who actually walk the walk; and all my T'ai Chi Chih friends.

Ginni Stern; France O'Brien; Kathleen Kehoe; Gary Alexander; Steve and Ginny Martinowitz; Diane Desmond and Russ Kinsley, for providing the soundtrack to these stories; Jody Petersen; Tim Brookes; Peter Kurth; Katharine Montstream and Al Dworshak; Diane, Liz and Dave Sander.

Nance Nahmias of South Burlington Barnes & Noble; Elaine Sopchak of the Book Rack in Essex; Karen Cady of Burlington Borders; Linda Lucey of Manchester (NH) Barnes & Noble; Barbara Ebling of Briggs Carriage in Brandon; the indomitable Elizabeth Orr of Burlington's Everyday Bookshop; Jim Brooking and Beth McElroy; Chris and Helen McCabe; and Steve Costello (fan #1).

Erik Esckilsen, writer extraordinaire, who has always treated me as a peer, thereby endlessly boosting my confidence.

And regarding Don Sander, I'm grateful more than I can say — and I can say a lot. When this man is in your corner, you feel like you're Muhammad Ali. For the first few years of the "Hackie" column, Don spent countless hours helping me edit each and every story. But, beyond all of this, I'm just proud to call him my friend.

Contents

Foreword BY KRISTIN D'AGOSTINO

Despite the fact that I hailed numerous cabs in Burlington trying to meet him, Jernigan Pontiac managed for months to elude me, like a cleverly disguised bank robber. At the time his newspaper column "Hackie" ran regularly in *Vermont Times,* where I'd begun working as a college intern, and I followed it with the loyalty of a daytime soaps fan. I'd been waiting to meet Jernigan at the office, thinking that eventually he'd have to come in to collect a paycheck or drop off his writing. But, no; being a free-wheeling columnist, Jernigan Pontiac was like a diaphanous phantom, conducting his earthly business at odd hours and possessing neither desk nor telephone extension.

I'd almost given up when, one day, in line at a local chocolate shop, a Canadian tourist asked me for directions. I was doing my best Map Quest impersonation when the man behind me gently interrupted in a Brooklyn accent: "Oh, no, there's a quicker way to get there. I only know 'cause I'm a *cabbie.*"

I don't know what clued me in, but something made me ask: "*You wouldn't happen to be . . .* ?" And the cabbie answered that, yes, as a matter of fact, he was. Just like that, in a serendipitous wink of an eye, my search was over.

The way our paths crossed seems *apropos,* given that part of what makes Jernigan's cab driving stories so riveting is their celebration of people meeting through chance. Townies, tourists and late-night revelers who, sprawled in the upholstered purgatory of his cab, moving between origin and destination, feel inclined to share their own unique histories.

In this, his second collection of stories, Jernigan Pontiac has established himself as Vermont's own Garrison Keillor, telling the strange, funny and touching tales that make up the heartbeat of the small New England city he and I know and love. Within the pages of this book, readers are given a sneak peak into Jernigan's rear-view mirror, where the hazy details of his passengers' lives gradually come into focus.

Like a graffiti artist spelling out the cities' inner musings, Jernigan combines personal reflections with bits of Vermont history and snippets of road-bound conversation to create meaningful stories about the human condition. Listening to his soulful inner monologue as he goes about his daily route is akin to witnessing a Brooklyn-born cabbie channeling Socrates, the Dalai Lama and Jimmy Breslin all at the same time. The result is an endearing mixture of poetry, sardonic wit and street smarts.

After finally meeting Jernigan, I often spotted his cab cruising around the Burlington streets. Seeing the illuminated taxi light gave me the warm feeling that everything was all right at that very moment, at least in one small corner of the world. People were being transported from place to place, and Jernigan was there in the thick of it, like some kind of guardian storyteller, watching over them and recording the fleeting echoes of their diverging lives.

Introduction

My good friend, Don Sander — a practical and clear thinker if there ever was one — says this about "finding oneself": If ever you find yourself confused about your values or life's path, simply gaze back and review the life you've lived.

Every individual's philosophy of life is written, as indelibly and profoundly as in any Biblical, Koranic or Vedic parchment, in the myriad large and small choices associated with daily living. Accordingly, so says Sage Don, you can stop fretting about discovering your "true calling." Fact is, for better or worse, you're living it.

The older I get, the more I've come around to Don's point of view. I'm a cab driver, a "hackie," to use the antediluvian word that so appeals to me. Wow! There's a certain AA-type liberation in that public admission: *My name is Jernigan, and I am a hackie.*

Mine is not the sexiest profession, not the career a mother dreams for her child. Hacking involves long hours, low pay and even lower social prestige. But unless I want to fall back on the repercussions of childhood misfortune or past-life karma, this is, in truth, the life I've chosen. No one has held a gun to my head, and said, "Drive or die."

So, what does this career choice, and the way I go about it, say about my values, what I hold dear, the things I find meaningful?

The stories contained in this volume hold the answer to this question. For nine years and counting — and for the last six in a column published fortnightly in the stellar Vermont newspaper *Seven Days* — I've been chronicling my cab-driving adventures in and around beautiful Burlington, Vermont. I pen these stories as much for myself as for my readers. They reveal to me who I am, what I believe in, what counts in my world.

As I look back over these tales, one dominant theme emerges — I seem to be learning a single lesson time and time again. It's an old teaching, one that Philo of Alexandria enunciated so succinctly a couple thousand years ago: "Be kind, for everyone you meet is fighting a great battle."

At least until I get it right — that is, fully absorb this lesson — I believe I'm destined to carry on with this cab-driving life. Which is not the worst fate I could imagine, particularly if writing about it remains part of the package.

Jernigan Pontiac
Spring 2006

1

HEARTS OF GOLD

If you're paying attention at all, it's hard not to recoil at the callous nature of this world. Greed abounds, increasingly on a global scale, as does its self-justifications. Anything goes; anything, that is, except acknowledging and truly caring for those with the least.

In the throes of this heartless landscape, now and then a sprinkling of quiet, benevolent people reveal themselves like succulent sprigs in an arid desert. You need to keep your eye out, though, because souls like these generally operate on the down-low, humility being the flipside of true compassion. Making a connection with a person of this caliber, even once a month, helps me keep the faith.

Perfect Autumn

Perched next to me, all five feet and 91 years of her, was a favorite regular customer. Rolling down 89 south out of Milton, the trees were lit up in welcome early October sunshine. How many straight days of gorgeous weather will we see this foliage season? The Vermonter in me can't help but think the Gods of Weather will extract payment for this preternaturally perfect autumn. But good weather in Vermont, like life in general, is best taken with an appreciative attitude, and I wasn't about to look a gift horse in the mouth. As I soaked in the glorious day, I would have been hard-pressed to name a person with whom I'd rather share this beautiful ride than Faith Reynolds.

"I just don't know, Jernigan."

Faith spoke to me with a clarity and force which belied her multitude of years on the planet. For the first time in her life, she explained to me, she had been experiencing a lot of unsteadiness, and the doctors couldn't seem to help.

"I think just maybe this will be my last year up here," she said.

Like many older Vermonters, Faith spends the colder months in Florida, on the Gulf Coast side so favored by our state's version of the snowbird. I've developed a theory about this. While Vermonters clearly enjoy their respite from the winter freeze, the truly hot temperatures they would encounter in the Miami area would be disorienting for people with a lifetime of Vermont winters in their cells and bones. The 60s-to-low-70s of the Tampa/ St. Pete region are, on the other hand, just about right.

I've driven Faith for a number of years to and from Burlington Airport on her yearly migration. In my 25 years living here, I've observed that Vermonters tend to be private by nature, at least until they get to know you. Perhaps Faith and I are temperamentally attuned, or perhaps I slowly wore down her resistance via the ancient and esoteric technique of Chat Kwon Do, in which I've earned my black belt. In any event, we've had quite the talks through the years, and "privileged" is not too strong a word to express my feeling about Faith's generosity in sharing her life stories with me.

As a girl growing up in Proctor, Vermont, Faith was sharp-minded, inquisitive and ambitious — traits not generally encouraged nor rewarded in the young women of that bygone era. Nonetheless, her parents supported her proclivities and, after high school, she attended Mt. Holyoke College in western Massachusetts. Upon earning her degree, she boldly set off for an office position in New York City. In short order, she met and wed her husband, Gerard, and the two of them made a life together in a mid-size town in upstate New York. Soon they had a bunch of kids. The family home was in a quiet neighborhood a few miles from the chemical manufacturer for whom Gerard worked as a salesman.

Gerard deeply loved Faith; *ipso facto*, he loved Vermont. It was his one regret that his job required residence near the plant, otherwise this Vermonter-of-the-soul would have surely moved his family to the Green Mountains. As the best consolation, they purchased the camp in Milton when the kids were young, and the family summered there without exception. Gerard's passing in 1982 didn't curtail this venerable family tradition.

"I noticed back at the camp you haven't sold the Volkswagen," I said. At the summer house, Faith kept a faded, yellow VW Bug, purchased new by she and her husband in 1966. Up until recent eye problems, she would tool around Milton in it.

"Oh, yes," Faith replied. "My neighbor Joe Beliveau took out the battery for safekeeping. He looks after the camp for me during the winter, don't you know."

Joe is among a number of camp residents who out of neighborliness, respect and, I've got to believe, sheer love, help out Faith in any way they can.

It was warm enough to have the window cracked, and the piercing squawk of a crow pulled our attention to the left. The big, black bird had just taken wing, but it seemed his vocal signal was to alert us to a particularly spectacular cluster of maples on the bluff of a passing hillside. The two of us wordlessly took in the impressionistic splash of pastel peach, orange and red. Amidst this bounty of color, I noticed a single tree, leafless and stark. Was it dead or just in early winter hibernation?

A few contemplative moments passed until Faith broke the reverie. "Do you remember my neighbor, Patty? She passed this summer."

One thing I've learned about old age from Faith is the recurring reality of losing friends. At this point, Faith is pretty much the oldest person among her various circles of acquaintances. Patty was an old dear friend whom she'd known for 50 years. The way Faith speaks of such matters is telling. She's neither maudlin nor morose; self-pity is simply foreign to her character. Rather, she speaks of life, unadulterated and real. She mourns her lost companions, and life goes on.

At the airport, I carried Faith's remarkably small amount of luggage — at this stage of the game, she's learned to travel light — into the terminal. I waited with her in the ticket line and then escorted her up to the waiting room. As we said our good-byes, Faith pondered aloud the very real possibility that this visit was her swan song to Vermont. She looked at me with pale, yet radiant eyes, which shone with a deep and still glow.

"Jernigan, thank you for everything," she said.

Pointedly missing was, "See you next year." That doesn't mean I wouldn't, but still I wiped tears from my eyes as I returned to the taxi and slowly pulled away from the curb.

The trees in Vermont just kill me. From the tiny, lime green leaves of verdant spring, into midsummer's lush, dewy jade — the entire cycle of transformation is thrilling. But how uniquely moved I find myself in early October, in the face of the sublime height of foliage beauty.

Last month a friend told me this about the maple trees: Their brilliant colors are there from the start, only fully revealing themselves as the green fades — in the autumn, before they die.

Mondo Bondo

I pulled my taxi into the driveway of a multi-dwelling home in the South End and honked once. Seconds later, a burly, red-haired man stepped out the side-porch door. He had strong, well-defined features on a ruddy face replete with laugh lines. Smiling broadly, he held up one index finger.

"We'll be out in one minute, Jernigan," he called out.

"Don't rush it, King Bondo," I replied. "I'm not going anywhere."

Fall is a transition time for this long-time and favorite customer of mine. I think at one point I learned his actual name, but I've long since forgotten it. King Bondo is a strange nickname for a person who conducts himself with a lot of humility, and not at all imperiously. Then again, there is something commanding and noble about his presence. Anyway, everyone calls him "King Bondo," so King Bondo it is.

He operates a small company providing landscaping services when it's warm and snowplowing when it's cold. The landscaping work is steady all summer, but in the winter the guy literally prays for snowstorms and plenty of them. He has contracts with dozens of people, mostly business owners, to plow their lots and driveways whenever there is a snowfall of a certain minimum height, I think six inches. I've seen him and his crew work nonstop for over 24 hours during blizzards. They do a great job — thorough and professional — and rack in the dough. But no snow means no plowing, and no plowing means no revenue.

In the building's parking area I saw the King's two massive, gleaming pick-up trucks — the guy is nothing if not impeccable in the care of his equipment. The vehicles sat there, at the ready, like a pair of lions awaiting the hunt; you'd half expect someone to come out and toss these beasts a few slabs of steak. It still being autumn, the truck beds were filled with various yard implements, stray mulch and limestone. Before long, I mused, the big plows would be hitched to their front ends.

Two other guys came down the steps and hopped in the back seat. "Hey Georgie, hey Slatter," I greeted them. These were King's two right-hand men. I believe one or both of them actually lived with King in the apartment.

"Hey, Jernigan," Slatter replied. "King Bondo'll be right out. You know how he is — he's got to get his hair just right when we hit the town."

"Is that right?" I said. "I'll be sure to give him grief about it."

King came bounding out and into the shotgun seat. "Gentlemen, let's do it!" he said, addressing his crew in the back. "Jernigan, the Sirloin Saloon, if you'd be so kind."

"Sure thing, King Bondo. And I'd be remiss if I didn't mention just how lovely your hair is this evening."

King spun in his seat and playfully cuffed first Georgie and then Slatter on the sides of their heads. Then facing forward again he reached up and shifted the rear mirror to view his reflection. "You're right, man. My hair does look quite lovely tonight."

"I'm going for the prime rib," Georgie offered as we turned south on Shelburne Road. "No question about it, I can use it."

"You deserve it, Georgie — no question about *that*. That was one big job today, and you guys worked your asses off. Whaddaya say we start with scallops as an appetizer? I'm jonesing for those babies."

King Bondo takes his crew out every so often, mostly to the Sirloin Salon, and he always covers the whole tab. The way these guys eat and drink, each one of these junkets costs him well over a 100 dollars. I know — from how he treats me — that he's laying huge tips on the wait staff as well.

"How's the winter shaping up?" I asked. "Have your old customers begun to call?"

"Yeah, I expect the plowing to be as busy as ever — so long as the snow flies, but don't get me started on that. Anyway, Jernigan, did I tell you? This is my last season. I'm going back to school."

I felt a pang. I abhor change, especially when it involves people I know. "You're kidding!" I replied. "You've been at this for years. You got a great business built up."

"That's true, and that's what made it a tough decision. But I'm in my thirties now, and I've always wanted to go into engineering. I'm talking to VTI, and I think I'll begin in the spring semester. Slatter's going to take the rigs and continue the business."

"Well, good for you, man. Good for you too, Slatter."

"Thanks, man," Slatter said, reaching forward and patting me on the shoulder.

The big red neon sign came into view — "Steaks, Seafood & Smiles" — and I took the left turn coming to a stop at the restaurant's wrap-around porch. I didn't feel much like smiling. The Vermont Technical Institute's in Randolph, so another customer was about to bite the dust. It's not the lost revenue but the camaraderie of King Bondo that I was going to miss — I was feeling it already. It seems like I've become a big softy, and that's fine with me. With age, the hard edges are wearing away. It's like the Dylan lyric, "I was so much older then, I'm younger then that now."

The fare for the three of them was ten dollars. The King gave me a twenty, a big smile, and said, "It's all you, Jernigan."

I took it, nodded my head and met his eyes. "No, brother," I said. "It's all you."

True Buds

It was the reunion weekend for St. Michael's College, and the downtown streets were jam-packed with alums trying to relive the glory days. I'd been driving them for hours, mostly to and from their hotel rooms. With the combination of still plentiful leaf-peepers and the ever-dependable locals, the night was shaping up nicely. Cab driving is wearying work under any circumstance, but the prospect of a good take keeps you coming back for more. I enjoy hacking as much as any cabbie — maybe more — but I'm not out there as a public service.

As I approached the Sweetwaters corner, I was hailed by two young men with "Boston St. Mike grads" written all over them. One of them wore a Red Sox cap, the other a hat with the logo of Legal Seafood, a popular Boston eatery. I pulled up to a double-parked stop and the Red Sox guy approached my window.

"We got a wheelchair, is that OK?" he asked, gesturing towards the sidewalk. There sat a young man in a compact, very aerodynamic-looking black wheelchair. The guy with the Legal Seafood hat was walking back to him.

"Jeez, I'd like to help," I said, "but my trunk is filled with stuff."

This was true. I had been helping a friend move earlier that day and some of his boxes remained in the trunk for unloading the next day. It was also true that I was relieved to have an excuse; the night was hopping, and I didn't want to spend the extra time involved in transporting a handicapped person.

"No problem, bro," the guy said. "We'll fold it into the back seat. We're headed to the Day's Inn across from St. Mike's."

"All right," I said. "If you think that's doable, let's get to it."

"Smitty!" he called to his friend on the sidewalk. "Wheel Brian over — the cabbie says it's a go."

"Ten-four, Jason," Smitty replied and rolled Brian towards the cab, slowing the chair down as they dropped off the curb. "You all set, Brian?" he asked. Brian nodded his head. Then, as Jason held the chair in place, Smitty slid one hand under Brian's thighs and the other around his shoulder and under his arm. He then lifted him out of the chair and gently eased him onto the front seat. It didn't look like a strenuous effort on Smitty's part; although of average height, Brian's torso appeared scrawny, his lower body almost weightless.

Meanwhile, Jason had popped off the wheels and placed them on the floor in the back of the cab. He then folded up the chair itself and slid it onto the back seat. Though obviously designed for maximum compactness, the chair still took up about two-thirds of the seat. Then playfully griping, Jason and Smitty squeezed into the remaining rear seat space. These two were clearly old pals and didn't mind the cramped quarters.

Before getting underway, I glanced over at Brian and noticed his fingers were curled and his hands bent sharply at the wrists. "Hey, man," I said, "could I help ya with the seat belt?"

"Thanks," he replied. "That would be great."

I reached over his shoulder, pulled the seat belt across his body and snapped it into place. The way he adjusted his body as I performed this maneuver told me he was accustomed to receiving this kind of assistance. "Thanks," he said, smiling as we got rolling.

"Brian, you stupid bastard!" Jason yelled at him from the back seat. "How many of those shots did you drink tonight? What'd ya think — we were back at Blarney's?"

"A few, I guess," Brian replied with a chuckle. He had a calm, quiet voice. I couldn't guess the full nature of his physical impairments, but I sensed a depleted energy level, like he couldn't speak loudly even if he wanted to. "It's a shame about the Blarney Stone," he continued. "That was the classic St. Mike's bar, wasn't it?"

"It was a fuckin' toilet," Smitty chimed in. "One of those places you love as a college student, but when you come back you go, "What the *hell* were we thinking?"

"Yeah, you're right," Jason said. "It was, like, a total dive. But, man, we had some wicked good times at that place."

We passed over the Williston Road cloverleaf and got on the highway. It was one of those crisp, clear autumn nights, the Milky Way twinkling overhead as we motored along. In a moonless sky, the stars were brilliant despite the dulling effect of the Burlington city lights.

"Cards tonight, Brian?" Smitty asked. "And don't say no, you friggin' asshole. You took enough off us last night."

"Sure, Smitty," my seatmate replied. "You want to donate more to the cause, I'll be glad to oblige."

We turned into the entrance at the Day's Inn and pulled to a stop. I shifted the vehicle into park because I knew this would take a while. Jason pulled the wheelchair out of the cab and reattached the wheels. "Hey, buddy," he asked Brian as Smitty lifted him from his seat, "which way do you like the cushion? I can't tell if I have it upside down or what."

"No, that's right the way you got it," Brian replied from his temporary perch in Smitty's arms.

Jason then paid the fare, and the three friends, still laughing and razzing each other, disappeared into the hotel.

The tenderness with which this pair of gruff Boston guys cared for their immobile friend stayed with me the rest of the night. I don't think I'd ever heard someone called a "stupid bastard" and "friggin' asshole" with such undeniable love.

New Year's News

It was New Year's Eve — the busiest night of the year for cabbies with no close second. I was flat out when a call came in from the Amtrak station.

"There's two of us out here who need a ride," a woman said. "I have to get to the Day's Inn, and there's a young woman who needs to get to some place called the Lund Home."

"Yep," I replied, "I know where both those places are at. I'll be out there in about 15 minutes and I can take both of you."

As I sped toward Essex Junction I thought about how enormously our cultural mores have changed since the Lund Family Center was founded so many years ago. Most people still call it the "Lund Home," which I believe was short for the "Lund Home for Unwed Mothers." But some things never change. There are still young women in need of sanctuary, and the Lund Home provides it when they're at their most vulnerable.

As I came upon the train station, a black woman of about 40 waved to me. On the ground next to her was a small, tan valise and in one hand she held a shopping bag overflowing with gold-wrapped boxes. She was plump — and I've got to say pleasingly so — and wore a violet hooded coat that offered some comfort on what was turning out to be an unusually rainy final day of the year.

"Hey, thanks for coming," she said as I pulled up next to her. "I'll go into the terminal and get the girl."

I loaded the woman's bags into the trunk and she returned carrying a bulky gym bag. Behind her walked a teenager, no more than 16, with bright rosy cheeks. She had a tiny, sleeping baby in a carrier.

The older woman got in the front with me, while the young mom climbed into the rear and seat-belted her infant. As we got underway, the woman pivoted to face the back and said, 'How are you doing, honey?"

"Oh, I'm doing great. Michele slept the whole way up on the train. She's such a good baby — I know I'm really lucky. That was awesome of you to get the cab for us. The station guy said it was gonna be a hard night to get one out here."

"That's fine dear," the woman replied. "You just keep taking good care of that baby. She is a darlin'."

"You staying in town for a few days?" I asked my seatmate.

"No, I'm renting a car tomorrow and driving out to spend time with my daughter. She just got married and moved to Hardwick. The Christmas gifts are a little belated, but I know she and her new husband will appreciate them."

The Day's Inn across from St. Michael's College came up on the left, and we pulled around the back to the lobby entrance. The woman and I got out, and as I unloaded her stuff from the trunk, she asked, "How much is my fare and hers combined?"

"Well, yours is $10 and hers will be $14. Are you gonna cover her fare?"

"Yes I am," she said, handing me a ten and a twenty. "Keep the change. Happy New Year."

"That is really, really something," I said, somewhat bowled over. "Thanks a lot."

"Hey, I've been there," she replied with a warm smile, and turned to walk into the hotel.

I got back into the driver's seat and we pulled away. "Guess what?" I said to the girl. "That lady just paid your fare."

"Omigod! That is totally sweet. I can't tell you how much that helps me out. I really needed the cab fare to buy diapers. I wish I could thank her. If you see her again, please tell her I said thanks."

"I sure will," I replied, thinking that's never going to happen.

A half-hour later I received another call from the train station. "Could you take me to the Sheraton?" a woman asked. "I was supposed to be picked up to go to Killington, but there's been a mix-up and I need to stay overnight at the Burlington Sheraton."

On my way back to Essex Junction the cellular rang again. "Hi, you gave me your card when you dropped me off at the Day's Inn. I called my daughter in Hardwick and she suggested I eat at Leunig's restaurant tonight."

"I'm on my way," I replied, and hustled out to first grab the Amtrak fare, which turned out to be a very stylish, thirty-something New York City woman. On the way to the Sheraton, we stopped at the Day's Inn to pick-up the Good Samaritan lady who again sat in the front with me. I spoke up right away.

"So, that young mother was quite touched by your generosity, paying her fare and all, and she said to tell you thanks."

"Look," the woman said. "When I was not much older than her, the father of my child walked out on us. it was right around Christmastime, and I didn't have a penny to my name. A neighbor came by one night with a holiday card. When she left, I opened it and there were three $100 bills inside. That allowed us to have Christmas, and I've never forgotten how much that meant to me."

First stop was the Sheraton, and I got out to unload the New York lady's suitcase and skis. She handed me $25."This'll cover both of us?" she asked.

"Don't tell me you're paying *her* fare?" I asked, now truly amazed. She had obviously overheard the story of the earlier ride. "That is too much."

"No it isn't," she shot back, and I could detect a touch of that Big Apple swagger. "Buddy-boy, that's just the way it's done."

I floated back into the cab, feeling like I was in a movie, except you couldn't make this stuff up. "Ma'am," I said, "you won't believe this, but that lady just paid *your* fare." The woman smiled, nodded her head once and didn't say a word.

The news of the world had begun to dampen my spirits of late, but these two magnificent women made me feel there was hope yet for the new year.

Waitress Tips

I pulled into Handy's downtown general store with something from the chocolate food group on my mind. A woman walked up to me as I stepped out of the cab and asked if I was working. I told her I was and she said, "Great. I need a ride after I pick up a few things at the store. I live up on North Prospect."

I was in and out quickly, Kit Kat in hand. I got back in the cab and sat there waiting for the woman, happily munching. She returned in a few minutes accompanied by another, older woman carrying a shopping bag in each hand. "I ran into my friend Natalya at Handy's," the younger woman said. "We'll drop her off on the way to my place if that's all right for you."

I got out again to help Natalya with her bags. She said thanks, which she pronounced, "danks," as I took them from her and placed them in the front seat. Turning back to assist her into the cab — she was moving with noticeable effort — I observed the dark blue bandana on her head. It covered most of her hair save for a few stray wisps of gray poking out from the sides. *Very Eastern European*, I thought to myself.

She smiled at me warmly as she took my arm, stepped into the back of the vehicle and took a seat next to her friend. Tiny lines surrounded her lips and she had a small scar over her left eye, yet Natalya's face was still pleasing, easy to look at. As a young woman, I thought, I bet she was a real beauty. It's just been a hard life. You could tell.

"Janice, thank you so much for this ride," Natalya said to her seatmate as we pulled out onto South Winooski Avenue. "You are such a sweetheart."

"Don't even say a word," Janice replied. "I'm more than happy to help out. You shouldn't be walking home all the way to Loomis Street. More important, how are feeling, dear? What do the doctors say?"

Natalya shook her head and made a clicking sound with her tongue against the roof of her mouth. "What do they know?" she said. "It's in God's hands; that's where I put my faith — in God's will."

"Well, amen to that, but you better be taking care of yourself. OK? Do what the doctors tell you. I don't want to miss you at Henry's Diner, even one morning. Your smiling face makes my day, you know that?"

In the rearview, I watched Natalya take Janice's arm in both hands and give it an affectionate squeeze.

When we arrived at Natalya's apartment, Janice lightly tapped on my shoulder, pointed to herself and mouthed, "I'll take care of it." I went around to help Natalya out of the cab and set her up with her bags. From the sidewalk, she gave a wave to Janice and said, "I'll see you for my coffee tomorrow." Janice smiled and blew her a kiss through the window.

"Poor woman," Janice said as we got back underway to her apartment. "I think it's some kind of stomach cancer. The doctors can't do much for her. She's a sweet lady, too. For years, she's been coming into the diner where I wait tables. It's a real shame."

We continued down Loomis Street. It was that dismal, post-foliage time of year. There were still some withered leaves skittering around the streets, but the trees were nearly bare. On the sidewalk, a couple of students scurried up towards campus clutching their coats against a stiff November wind.

"You know," I said, "it feels colder this time of year than it does in the heart of winter. It's just so bleak. What's it — four o'clock or so? It's already dark, for Pete's sake."

"Yeah, I know what you mean," Janice said. "When the snow falls it seems to cheer things up. The white coat is like a frosty blanket." She paused for a moment and scrunched her face. "Frosty blanket? That don't make much sense, huh?"

"It makes sense to me," I replied with a chuckle. "But, of course, most of my friends say I'm goofy, so . . ."

"Well, this *is* Vermont," Janice continued. "That's what I tell my customers. It's like life — things aren't always sunny and warm and pleasant, so there's no reason the weather should be."

"I like your analysis, Janice. That's what I'm gonna tell my customers from now on when they get whiny about the cold."

When we reached North Prospect Street, she had me take a right and pull in front of one of the buildings along a stretch that has been subdivided into small apartments. She said, "I'm around the back, but you can just drop me here. How much do I owe you for both of us?"

"How about six?" I replied.

"For both me and Natalya? Should be more than that."

"Well, tough luck, 'cause I say it's six."

Janice smiled and handed me a five and a one. Then she pulled out another five and passed it over, saying, "That's for you, honey."

I headed back downtown thinking to myself, *I just love waitresses. I really, really do.*

Inside Information

The Vermont Transit driver stepped out of his bus and motioned me over. *This is unusual,* I thought. I know most of the drivers by sight, and once in a while we exchange a nod or a wave, but why request a *tête-á-tête*?

I strode over and the guy put his hand on my shoulder. "I have a couple here who need to get to Howard Johnson's."

I said, "That's cool . . ."

"But here's the thing," he continued. "They're blind and deaf."

"Holy smoke! How do you communicate with them?"

"Easy," the driver replied, "You take the guy's palm and spell out what you want to say." His broad smile made me think he had enjoyed his time on the bus with these folks. "It works really well."

First their dog emerged down the three bus steps — a large yellow lab, the breed often used for seeing-eye duty. The couple followed — mid-thirties, casually dressed like typical tourists. The man was compact and bald, with a neatly-trimmed goatee, and he comfortably held the leash handle attached to his dog's body harness. His companion was a fair-skinned woman with an aquiline nose and fine, light-brown, shoulder-length hair. *A nice couple*, I thought to myself.

I took the man's palm in my left hand, and with my right forefinger wrote out, "HI." He smiled and nodded a few times. Meanwhile a bus terminal employee — one of the men who handle the luggage and freight — had carried the couple's three bags over to my cab and was placing them into the open trunk. My customer made a small grunting sound to get my attention, and then mimed with his hands the outline of a small case. I got what he was saying, and took his hand and spelled, "OK." Then I removed the smallest suitcase from the trunk and brought it back to him. He took it under one arm, smiled and nodded.

Following my lead, the dog then guided the two of them to my taxi. The pooch got in first, hopping into the back seat, followed by the couple. The man then reached into his case and passed me a piece of paper with the hotel written on it, along with its Shelburne Road address. I took his hand and again spelled, "OK." This *was* enjoyable.

As we drove south on Shelburne Road, the two of them talked and laughed in the back seat. I say "talked and laughed" because that's what it looked and felt like to me as I glanced into the rear-view mirror and watched the dancing hands. There was not a sound but for the occasional grunt from him or small yelp from her. I couldn't say exactly how they were communicating, but they appeared to be employing conventional sign language with this twist: Rather than seeing the hand movements, they held each other's hands to feel the shapes. It was beautiful and magical to behold.

As anyone negotiating Shelburne Road this summer has experienced, it was stop-and-go amidst the road-widening construction, or as I call it, "Burlington's Big Dig." I began to think about my customers in the back, but my mind simply could not get around it. I'd been with people who are blind, and I'd been with people who are deaf. Either one of these missing faculties I could grasp. But both? What was their world like?

A flag-person up ahead raised her stop sign, and I slowed to a halt in a line of waiting cars. I placed the taxi in park and jammed my thumbs firmly into my ears. Then I shut my eyes tight and held this position for maybe 10 seconds. I was floored; all I can say is, try it.

The traffic line restarted, and we soon came upon the hotel. I took the left and stopped at the front entrance. Reaching back over the seat, I took the man's hand and spelled out, "WAIT I'LL GO IN." He nodded his assent.

I ambled up to the young woman behind the front desk. "I'm bringing in a couple of folks. I'm guessing you're expecting them; they're both deaf and blind."

"No, not really," the woman said with a look of mild alarm. She rallied immediately, though. "But this is not a problem. Bring 'em on in; we'll take good care of them."

When I returned to the cab the couple had already gotten out. I attempted to lead them through the front door, but the dog was intent on pulling the man off to the side. I figured the critter was disoriented from the long journey, and I tried to gently steer the guy in my direction. It was man vs. dog for the stewardship of his master. Finally, the man shook free of my grip, and raised his arm, palm facing me. He then followed the animal's lead over to a small flower bed, where the doggie relieved himself.

Canine bathroom needs satisfied, our group entered the hotel and approached the front desk. I took the opportunity to go back outside to fetch the luggage. When I returned, my female customer had placed a small device on the desk between herself and the front-desk person, which the two of them were now employing to communicate. It looked like a pair of small, connected keyboards and somehow — I couldn't quite figure it out — it allowed them to "talk."

The man must have sensed my presence, because he got my attention and rubbed his thumb and fingers together in the universal semaphore, "How much?" I spelled out the number "NINE," and he removed a 10-dollar bill from his wallet, signaling me to keep it. I took his hand and spelled, "THANK YOU," and then, in a moment of I-don't-know-what, I added, "PEACE." He smiled at me warmly.

I drove away feeling like I had been with holy people, and weeks later I still feel touched by the experience. True, I get to witness sunsets over Lake Champlain, and to hear cardinals and Beethoven and gurgling babies. But I sense there's something unfathomably rich — perhaps even limitless — about the inner world in which these two courageous people dwell.

One Voice for Peace

"Thank you veddy much," said Mr. Bakri as I helped him into the front seat. It was last year, late summer.

This elderly customer of mine was impeccably mannered. In his dress, his speech, his every movement, he embodied the graciousness of an old-world gentleman. In his case, the old world was post-World War II Beirut. Prior to Lebanon's mid-'80s political breakdown and ensuing chaos, Beirut enjoyed a few precious decades of peace, prosperity and cultural flowering, earning the nickname "The Paris of the Mideast."

"Is there a tournament tonight?" I asked as we got underway.

"No, Jernigan, just the regular weekly match play."

For the better part of a year, I had been driving Mr. Bakri to his weekly games at the Burlington Bridge Club on Gregory Drive, just before the Williston town line. Given his humility, I had only recently discovered — from his adoring wife who occasionally accompanied him — that he was the top bridge player in the state.

"Mr. Bakri," I said, "forgive me if I already asked you this, but how did you become so accomplished at bridge? Have you been playing your whole life?"

"Well, I don't know how accomplished I am," he replied with customary modesty. "I'm still learning. But, yes, to answer your question — I've been playing bridge since I was a teenager in Palestine. But I've only seriously applied myself to the game since retirement. When I was running my little business there was no time for such frivolity."

"Little business," indeed. I'd had more than one discussion with Mr. Bakri about the export business he had founded in Beirut shortly after his family relocated there from Haifa during the war precipitated by the founding of Israel in 1948. His firm introduced frozen foods to the Arab world, distributing products such as South American lamb throughout the region. By the time he sold the company a decade ago, he had warehouses and operations on at least four continents. By any measure, it was a huge accomplishment for this soft-spoken man.

The Bakris appeared to live a relatively modest lifestyle — well below their means, one would imagine — residing in a condo a stone's throw from the Vermont National Country Club. The only extravagance, if you could call it that, I'd observed were the prepared meals regularly delivered to their home from an Arab restaurant in Montreal.

Politics was a topic I'd not before broached with this customer, but recent events in his erstwhile homeland had me interested in gaining his perspective. Normally, I avoid political discussions in the cab — or out of the cab, for that matter. Not that I'm indifferent; if anything, I'm too passionately concerned about the state of the world. But few people these days seem willing to engage in an open-minded dialogue about politics, resorting instead to well-worn ideological pronouncements. My feeling is, if you're not willing to be influenced by another — maybe (God forbid) modify your opinion — what's to discuss?

Mr. Bakri, however, was to my eyes a person whose thoughtfulness, seasoned by an uncommon integrity and clarity, had risen to the level of wisdom. As a middle-aged man still struggling to make sense of this world, I consider elders like Mr. Bakri to be jewels. So long as he seemed receptive, or at least not obviously resistant, I was going to do some mining.

We approached the airport, passing the Hooters restaurant under construction, a soon-to-be edifying addition to Burlington's cultural landscape. *Like your average male needs any* additional *sexual stimulation in his life,* breezed through my mind.

"So, have you seen the news lately?" I asked. "It looks like Sharon might actually relinquish the Gaza lands to the Palestinians. Do you think there's any reason for hope at this point?"

Mr. Bakri emitted an audible sigh as he turned his head to face me. "Jernigan," he said, "there is always hope. But it is up to both sides to renounce all violence, and consider the next generation, and the generation after that."

He paused for a moment to gather his thoughts, reaching up to smooth one of his eyebrows with the middle finger of his right hand. "There is so much anger, so much hatred on both sides. And with good reason — that's the tragic aspect."

Mr. Bakri had once told me, almost off-handedly, that prior to Israeli independence his father was the single-largest private landholder in all of Palestine, a man of enormous wealth and influence. The family's expulsion from their homeland effectively killed his father. If anyone had justification for hatred, it was Mr. Bakri.

"Yes, it's true," he continued, "my people — the Palestinian people — have been horribly mistreated for over 50 years. But the Jews, as well, have suffered terribly throughout all of their history, to say nothing of the Holocaust. So the only solution is for both people to stop it — stop the violence and the hatred, and work toward peace and mutual prosperity."

This was as passionate as I'd ever seen this man get. I felt a little guilty about disturbing his equanimity with my questioning. He then shook his head and said quietly, "That's all I can say about this."

I didn't know it at the time, but this to be my last ride with Mr. Bakri.

When a regular customer stops calling, often I'll know the reason. *Jernigan, guess what? I'm moving to Oakland in a couple of weeks.* Something like that gives me the heads up. Sometimes, though, the calls just cease and I'll be left wondering: *Did she finally get her driver's license back?* Or, perish the thought, *Did he switch to another taxi company?*

Mr. Bakri hadn't called for months, and I didn't know the reason. But recently, just by chance, I drove one of his neighbors who told me that he had passed away last fall. *Our world,* I thought, *has just lost a rare voice of reason.*

2

NINE ELEVEN

In the immediate aftermath, those first few weeks and months, no one was sure what to call it. Some people spoke of the "terrorist attack"; others, the "disaster," or "catastrophe." In time, it became simply, "9/11," — an antiseptic, oddly bloodless appellation for so cataclysmic and visceral an event.

The blow convulsed our world, unleashing a whirlwind that staggers us to this day. Remaining true to our core values in the face of such aggression has been a formidable challenge for all of us, as individuals and as a nation. And as the aftershocks careen throughout the culture, they often find their way into my taxi world.

After the Deluge

It was the first Friday, week one of the new world. I was in my taxi, out on the streets, still — inapposite as it seems — trying to make a living.

I remember when the Khmer Rouge took over Cambodia they imposed a new calendar, as if the nation's few thousand year history had ceased to exist and time was beginning anew. Had the terrorists who acted on September 11th achieved such a time stoppage? It felt that way to me, as if the life I knew last week had evaporated, and now existed only as a vaguely, if fondly, remembered dream.

I was called to a pick up at Vermont Transit to take a college student up to the freshmen dorms. Arriving at the bus terminal, I saw a young woman standing to the side, a single backpack slung over her shoulder. Her straw-colored hair was carelessly tied back in a long braid. She looked listless, almost shell-shocked.

"Hey, did you phone for the cab?" I called to her, pulling to a stop.

She nodded blankly, walked over and got in the front. As we got underway, ascending the hill, she suddenly looked familiar.

"Didn't I take you last Friday?" I asked. "What was it you told me — were you going down to New York City on account of a death in the family?"

"Yes, my grandmother died, and the funeral was last weekend. I was really close with her — it was just horrible. And then the terrorist attack . . ." A wave of distress came over her face. "This is the worst thing that ever happened in my life. I've had a stomach ache every morning for three days."

"It is a terrible thing," I agreed. "When I was a little kid — it must have been third grade — I remember the afternoon our teacher came into the room with tears streaming down her face. She was a beautiful old Irish lady, Mrs. Stroll, with a big bun of reddish-gray hair held aloft with a couple of antique silver clips. It's funny the things you remember. Anyway, she told the class that President Kennedy had been shot and killed, and then she broke into sobs. They closed the school and sent us all home. That's what this feels like now — it's that huge."

I glanced over at the young woman, and saw she was lost in her thoughts, not — or just barely — listening to my reminiscence. I didn't blame her; the events of this week were not *like* anything. The baby-boomer story that spilled out of me was just me trying to cope, to impose some perspective. In truth, I realized, there is no perspective to be had, at least for quite a while. There's just raw emotion, interspersed with varying degrees of numbness and diversion.

"What's going to happen now?" she turned to me and asked. She had little-kid eyes, beseeching and afraid. Sometimes I forget how young they are, the college kids, particularly the freshmen. The guys are mostly bigger and stronger than me, and the women are vivacious and womanly as they stride around town with purpose and intent. But really, they're only kids, barely out of high school, just flown from the protective nest of family and home.

"What do *you* think is gonna happen?" I said.

"I have, like, no idea. This dude sitting next to me on the bus kept talking about war, and how it's now our generation's chance to prove ourselves. He was sure there was going to be many more attacks like this week. Even worse maybe. I mean, what could be worse? That's, like, too sick to think about."

Ever since the disaster, I've been inundated with the television news at home, phone conversations with friends and relatives, along with the feelings and ideas of the customers I drive in my taxicab. The usual talk of weather and sports has ceased entirely, replaced by the only event that now seems to matter. What can I offer this pained young woman that won't land in her world as one more piece of overwhelming information?

"Well," I said, "this is what I've noticed. Everyone is going to have their own opinion, which is going to be colored by their personality and upbringing. It's like the whole country is in bereavement at the same time, just like you're going through with the loss of your grandmother. And we all grieve in different ways, and at a different pace."

"So who can you believe?" she asked. I could tell she was intently listening to me now — God help her — and her eyes focused on me like a beam of light.

"I think you have to figure it out for yourself. It's OK to listen to everyone's ideas and feelings — I think that's all part of the healing that's going on. But, at the end of the day, you got to come to your own conclusions.

Nobody knows where this is all going to lead, but we all have a choice of sticking to our deepest values, and not getting swayed by the anger and emotion of others."

We were stopped at the light at the turn onto Spear Street, just near her dormitory. I chuckled, and asked, "Is this helpful to you in the least? Am I making any sense? 'Cause you know, the crack cocaine is wreaking havoc with my coherence."

"Hey," she said, "Just say 'no.' Didn't your mama teach you anything?"

We both laughed. For me it was the first time in three long days. Maybe, I dared to hope, time hasn't stopped, and life will abide. Changed yes, but still connected meaningfully to our past, to our lives before Tuesday morning, September 11, 2001.

Hail to the Chief

A hand came up on the corner of Church and Main Streets, and I quickly shot over to secure the fare. No fooling around these days.

It's been slim pickings for us Burlington cabbies since the terrorist attacks last month. Fewer regulars and far fewer tourists are partaking in the local nightlife. Worse than that, at least for an independent driver like me who concentrates on downtown business, is the flood of airport-based cabbies suddenly omnipresent as new competition. Like bears forced into the city when the rural food source dwindles, the airport cabbies are starving from lack of sky travelers. I know most of these guys, and I sympathize with their plight. But as a consequence of their situation, I'm feeling the pinch.

The man who hailed me was holding hands with, presumably, a wife or girlfriend. With his free hand, he opened the front door and asked, "Can you take us to the Ethan Allen Motel?"

It always surprises me a little when people ask this type of question instead of just getting into the cab. I suppose they're being polite, like when you ask the general store guy, "Would you get me a pack of Marlboros?" What's he going to answer, "No, I don't think so?"

"Yup," I replied. "That's pretty much what I do for a living. If it's connected via land mass to Burlington, Vermont, I'm the right guy to take you there."

Am I droll or obnoxious? It's a fine line I lost track of long ago. In any event — like the song says — I gotta be me.

The guy smiled, and the two of them got in the back. They looked like a well-matched couple, definitely of the clean-cut mode. Underway I asked, "So how'ya enjoying your stay in Burlington?"

"Burlington's just great," the man replied. "Our cab ride downtown was atrocious, though. When the cab arrived to pick us up, my girlfriend was taking a minute finishing up in the motel room, and the cabbie stuck his head through his window and started barking at us to hurry up."

"Well, you know how that goes," I said. "Maybe he was having a rough night. I'm not excusing that behavior, though. There's no need to take it out on innocent customers."

"Now you're a much nicer cabbie," the woman injected. "Isn't he, dear?"

Her boyfriend chuckled. "Well he's not screaming at us, and that's a lot nicer, I guess."

"Yeah," I chimed in, "you haven't exactly set the bar all too high."

We were stopped at the Prospect Street light, at the top of the hill. In my mind, I was going over their crabby cabbie story. If I was that driver, I thought, I'd save my outbursts for customers who really deserve it, not the merely slow-movers.

"Hey, do you ever get up to St. J?" the woman asked, changing the subject.

"Maybe a couple of times a year, or so. Why do you ask?"

"Because this guy right here is the new Chief of Police of St. Johnsbury."

I glanced up at the rear-view mirror, and I could see the woman just beaming. The man was smiling, too, ear-to-ear.

"No kidding?" I said. "Congratulations, that's terrific. So tonight must be your celebration in the big city."

The new Chief didn't say a word, just smiled and nodded his head.

"If you don't mind me asking, you seem kinda young. How long have you been with the department?"

"Twelve years," he replied. "The force has about 11 full-time officers."

You could tell the guy was so proud, as well he should be. An entire community, the largest in the Northeast Kingdom, has placed its safety and protection in his hands. For somebody in law enforcement, what could be a greater recognition, or honor?

Since the disaster of 9/11, these matters of public protection are suddenly first and foremost. It's not just theoretical anymore; the bravery and sacrifice of those many firefighters and police officers at the World Trade Center have made it all too real. One would guess Vermont's Northeast Kingdom would be far down any fanatic's list of terrorist targets. But still, if the public security is under attack from any quarters, it's the local men and women in blue — like this soft-spoken new Chief sitting in the back of my cab — who stand ready to lay down their lives on our behalf.

I thought back to my rebellious youth, and how that version of myself would react to this appreciative view of the cops. Yet one more thing to add to that growing list: the changes of outlook that come with age.

"You know," I said, turning into the hotel at the illuminated silhouette of Ethan Allen, "if I'da known who I was dealing with, I might not have driven quite so fast up through the University."

"Don't sweat it," the Chief said, laughing. "I'm not working tonight, and besides, this ain't my jurisdiction!" He then took out a ten and handed it to me, adding, "Keep the change, and thanks so much for the ride."

"No, Chief," I replied. "Thank *you*."

Home Wrecker

"Well, this settles it," I said to my seatmate as we negotiated the myriad speed bumps which now line the North Champlain Street access to the Northern Connector. "You know, for years there's been this debate among us cabbies about the quickest route to the New North End. Some are of the North-Avenue-all-the-way school; others — like myself — favored the Connector. It's been a close call, but these God-awful speed bumps have tipped the scales. There's no justification for taking the Connector anymore unless you're headed all the way to Mallet's Bay."

I turned and glanced at my customer, a pale, thirty-something man with short, tightly curled brown hair and whopping lips, like two pieces of over-ripe red fruit. He grinned — facetiously I thought — and let out an extended froggy belch.

He had just polished off the last of a sausage sub that, before entering his body, had been piled high with peppers and onions and slathered in rust-colored barbeque sauce. From the time he entered the taxi, I had been watching him devour this meaty leviathan in a series of methodical swallows of python-like enormity. It was a gruesome performance and a part of me was repulsed. Another part of me, I'm not proud to say, was riveted.

Other than a mumbled Shore Road destination, my customer's *basso-profundo* burp was his first verbal offering since we'd gotten underway. I was prepared to take it as his last word on the speed-bump situation, but he had more to say on the subject.

"This is a joke," he said, straightening up in the seat and wiping his lower lip with a jacket sleeve. It was time to chat, apparently, now that dinnertime was over. "A total freaking joke," he continued. "They should bulldoze this whole decrepit neighborhood, from Champlain to Park Street. Then they could lay down a decent access road to the Connector. I mean, what's stopping them? This is a ghetto, for crying out loud."

After 25 years of hacking, nothing emerging from the mouth of one of my fares much startles me anymore, but Sausage Man's sentiments did take me aback. I said, "What about the people who — "

"Screw them! Screw the 'people.' D'ya know what kinda individuals live in these run-down shitboxes?"

This, I grasped, was a rhetorical question. It's a given that we all know what kind of people live in the Old North End — gypsies, tramps and thieves.

As I took the right onto the Connector (my last time on a North Avenue run, I'd decided), the clock turned to 12 midnight and the hourly news came on the radio. It was our Director of Homeland Security, the hopelessly unreassuring Tom Ridge, informing the nation what color to paint our fear this week. This was all the prompting my man required.

"Do you know what I say? I say, nuke 'em all! Iraq, Iran — this is all bullshit! These people hate us. It's us or them. I say, flatten the landscape. I'm talking about the surface of the moon. The world'll be a better place."

You got to hand it to him, I thought — the guy is nothing if not consistent. His solution to the problems of the world, be they bad roads or rogue states, is leveling the topography.

His were provocative, if not homicidal words, and I knew better than to retort. The guy was ranting and I've learned this about ranters — they're not open to discussion. So I bit my tongue. Prudent? Perhaps, but it didn't forestall my rising ire.

What had really pushed my buttons was not this person's malevolent views, but the insouciance with which he voiced them. His opinions came embedded with the galling assumption that I, the listener, naturally agreed with him. That got me thinking about the talk radio ranters — their propensity to say "we" when they mean "I," and their assumed mandate that they speak for the "people."

Nothing gets my goat like unbridled arrogance, my thoughts raced on. *What did the shrinks say in a recent study?* I tried to remember. Is *it healthier to express anger, or now are they saying it's better to repress it?* This guy had gotten to me, no doubt. By the time we turned onto Shore Road, small puffs of smoke were wafting from my ears.

He pointed out his house and I pulled into the driveway coming to stop. As he paid the fare, the same irksome smile was plastered on his face.

"You don't really agree with me," he said, to my surprise. "C'mon, tell the truth. You don't see things my way. Am I right?"

"No, now that you ask. You're right — I don't."

"All right, then," he said. There was relish in his words as he smacked his billowy lips. "What *do* you think?"

This stopped me in my tracks, and I hesitated before responding. Do I really want to get into it with this guy? Once I framed it that way, the answer came easily.

"To be frank, brother," I replied, meeting him eye-to-eye, "I don't believe you're truly interested in what I think, so I'm gonna pass."

The smile dropped from his face. I could tell he didn't expect *that* response. Then he burst out laughing, shaking his head back and forth and slapping his thigh.

"Ya know what?" he said. "You're absolutely right! I really could not care less what you think." He chuckled a few more times, and left the cab.

I sat there realizing that, in an odd way, he had gained a modicum of respect in my eyes with that closing remark. At least he was being honest, and that counts for something.

Warrior

Trolling for a fare downtown on a Saturday night, I noticed a man speaking with another cabbie idling at the curb up ahead. As I watched, the man shook his head, turned away from the parked cab and flagged me down. *This could be sketchy,* I thought to myself. There's usually a good reason when a cabbie turns down a fare, probably some variation of *I don't have any money on me, but when we get to my house . . .*

I pulled to a stop in traffic and turned on my four-ways. Lowering the passenger window, I asked, "Whadaya need, bud?"

"Do you know how to get to the Ethan Allen Firing Range?"

"Sure do," I replied. "It's out in Jericho. Ya need a ride there?"

"Thank goodness," he replied, climbing into the front seat. "This other cabbie had no idea how to get there."

"I think he's a new guy. We don't get a helluva lot of rides to the firing range. It's just that I've been on the job for about 100 years, so I tend to know where everything is."

"Is that so?" the guy said with a chuckle.

"Yeah, and it's not that I got a particularly sharp memory or anything. It's just a matter of time, volume and repetition."

In a block or two we left behind the Saturday night crowds, and as we ascended the Main Street hill I asked, "What brings you up here?" Before he could respond I remembered our destination, and quickly added, "You with the Guards?"

"That's right. I'm from Toledo. You know — Ohio. They sent me out for a 10-day training. Great town you got here."

"It works for me," I said. "Man, it must be a hairy time to be in the National Reserve. Guys are being sent over to Iraq left and right these days."

"Yeah, it's tough, but that's what you sign up for. If I gotta go, I'll go proudly. I'm 100% behind the cause."

"What's the cause?" I asked.

The question sounded flippant leaving my lips, but it was genuine. Like many other Americans, I feel like I've lost track. The invasion of Afghanistan I grasped: that country was clearly harboring the guys who attacked us. But I honestly did not understand what we're doing in Iraq. The soldier sitting next to me, however, had no doubts whatsoever.

"We're taking the war on terror to the bad guys on their own turf. It's either that or we have to fight 'em on American soil. We got Saddam, and when you cut off the head, the body shrivels up and eventually dies. So, like Bush says, we got to stay the course, and I'm ready to do my part."

Though I didn't see things his way, I was actually glad, for his sake, to experience the man's certainty. Everyone in the country has a stake in this issue, but for a person who might be called upon to serve in Iraq, it's literally a matter of life and death. I have an old friend whose tour of duty during the Vietnam years was fraught with ambivalence, and he's had to live with that his whole life. If this guy is called overseas, at least he's secure in his purpose.

At the Jericho fork in the road, I could see that Joe's Snack Bar was preparing to open for the season. I salivated at the thought of one of Joe's killer creemees, maybe a king-sized vanilla with chocolate jimmies. What a luxury, it struck me, to enjoy the small pleasures of spring, rather than to be crouched in a bunker with three other soldiers, or huddled in an apartment with a couple of your terrified kids watching for the next rocket propelled grenade.

We slipped onto the firing range access road and soon came to a manned checkpoint. This was new to me. Prior to September 11th — and I realized that this was my first trip out here since that transformative day — the security had been non-existent, at least as far as I could tell.

I pulled up to the booth and lowered my window. Before I could utter a word, my customer leaned forward and said, "Hey Dennis — how you doing, man?"

"Hey — what's up Jimmy? Run into any wild women downtown?"

"Too many to count, Dennis."

Dennis chuckled and turned his attention back to me. "Sir, could you show me some ID?"

I got out my license and passed it over. He looked at the picture, and looked at me. Carefully. He then looked back at the picture, handed it back and let us through.

The guy — who I now knew as Jimmy — guided me to his barracks. He paid the fare, plus a decent tip. "Thanks, man," I said, "and good luck."

Before closing his door, he paused for a moment as if there was something he wanted to say. He then said, "It's not that I'm raring to get into this fight over in Iraq. You know what I'm saying? It's just that this is the vow I made when I joined the military. It's my duty to our country, pure and simple."

"I hear what you're saying and I respect it entirely," I replied.

As I watched the guardsman make his way back into his sleeping quarters, I thought about the men in suits in Washington responsible for initiating and prosecuting this conflict. Our country can ill-afford to squander the patriotic ideals of people like Jimmy, but I fear we are doing exactly that. I really hope, though, that events prove me wrong.

Homecoming

The man in the back seat of my cab was angry at something, and I just hoped it wasn't me. He was of medium height, but built solid, like a brick: Well-defined muscles swelled from every area of exposed skin, including — most fearsome to me — his neck. "Tightly wound" was the phrase that came to mind; his voice constricted, his body language forced and ungraceful.

"Those spoiled bitches," he growled. "Who the hell do they think they are?"

"What'd you have a rough night in the clubs?" I asked.

"Those bitches!" he said, amping up the sentiment, essentially ignoring me. "Prancing around with daddy's credit card — think they're better than everyone."

Another local who's resentful of the college students, I thought to myself. Most of the college kids come from higher-income families, so the backdrop of class warfare is always part of the picture as they interact with the working-class population on bar nights. Add the sexual element into the mix and things can really get dicey.

In the rearview mirror I watched as the man lowered his window and scowled at the passing throngs. He appeared poised to hurl insults at random passersby, a nasty routine I just refuse to countenance. Drive-by belligerence is ugly, and I was not going to play wheelman if that's what the guy had in mind. *Never mind his intimidating physique,* I decided; *I'd confront him if it comes down do it.*

Then, just as abruptly, he re-closed his window and said, "I just got out of the service two days ago."

"Is that so?" I replied. "Were you overseas?" The conflagration that is Iraq immediately came to mind, but I couldn't bring myself to ask the question using the "I" word.

"That's right," he said. "I was in a Marine unit in Baghdad. Eight months. And I'm not talking about the Green Zone, either. We were constantly on patrol."

"Holy smokes," I said, momentarily stunned.

Like most everyone, the war in Iraq has been a part of my daily consciousness since it started. I've read about it, watched it on TV, heard it discussed on the radio and debated it with my friends. But the instant this soldier spoke, I realized how abstract my "experience" of the war had been. This guy had *been* there — fighting for eight months, no less.

We made our way to South Union and turned north towards an address on Archibald Street. The man suddenly lurched forward and rested his forearm across the top of the front seat. "Do you know what a 50-caliber round is?" he asked.

"Um, not really," I answered awkwardly. "Some kind of bullet, I guess."

"That's right," he said. "It's a bullet about this big." He stretched his right hand over the seat, his thumb and forefinger describing a spread of six or seven inches.

I glanced to my side to look, and said, "That's huge."

"That's right," he said again, as if praising a particularly bright 10 year-old. "I watched my best friend in the unit — a medic, name of Troy — blown to bits by that round."

"Christ. When did that happen?"

"Last month. You want to ask me what I think of the war?"

The man's intensity was unnerving to me. I wasn't exactly scared of him any longer, but this wasn't a comfortable conversation by any means. Yet, somehow, I felt it was my duty to listen to what he had to say, to bear witness. Regardless of my feelings about the war, this person had served in the American military and that means he's fought on all our behalf. This is not the way I would have looked at it in my younger years, but it's the way I see it now.

"Tell me, man," I said to him, "what do you think about the war?"

"Here's how it is: When the bullets are flying, there are no politics. You're just trying to stay alive another day."

We turned onto Archibald and I pulled to a stop in front of the man's place. I said, "I hope I'm not out of line saying this, but you've just been through some seriously hellacious experiences. You know there's counseling for vets at the VA office. I have a good buddy who saw a lot of death during his tour in Vietnam. He eventually made it into the VA and it helped a lot."

The guy's face dropped, and I could see the weariness, the despair beneath all the bitterness and bravado. "Well, I'll keep that in mind," he said, lifting out his wallet and paying the fare.

"*Semper Fi,*" he said, and closed the door behind him.

Semper Fi, I repeated the words to myself. Short for *Semper Fidelis,* the motto of the U.S. Marine Corps. I couldn't say where I learned this, but I believe it translates as "Always Faithful."

What a powerful maxim, I thought as I threaded my way back downtown. *Not unlike a wedding vow.* I wondered if the Marine Corps would reciprocate that loyalty now that he's done his duty and returned stateside? Will we?

3

WOMEN ON THE MOVE

A taxi ride is about physical movement from one point to another. Sometimes my customers also find themselves in another kind of transition, from one place in their lives to another. Who they are, or think they are, is in flux. Didn't the Buddha happen to mention that everything in life is impermanent?

Moms Gone Wild

Two women scurried up to my taxi as I idled for a moment after dropping a fare at Nectar's. They appeared somewhat older than your typical late-night bar-hoppers, but both were attractive women. By their beaming smiles, I could tell they'd enjoyed a fun night out together.

I lowered the passenger window and the shorter woman stepped up and asked, "Can you take us to Richmond?" She had short, honey-blonde hair and warm brown eyes. I hesitated for a moment, and her friend, a tallish brunette, chimed in, "Please Mr. Cabbie — the last two cabdrivers said they couldn't do it."

"Yeah," I said, "that figures. When it gets busy around last call, all the cabs want to stay local. Out-of-town fares actually cost money this time of night." I could see their faces start to drop. "But fear not," I quickly added. "I'll take you. I never turn down fares on that basis — I figure everybody needs to get home."

"Thank you, thank you, thank you," the blonde said and, giggling, they both jumped into the back seat.

"I can't remember the last time I had gravy fries, Janey," the blonde woman said to her friend as I wove my way out of downtown. "They were as gooey delicious as ever."

"I don't know how I let you talk me into that, Donna. I can feel my hips widening as we speak."

"Yup, those gravy fires have become quite the Burlington signature," I joined in. "One time I told a tourist that Nectar's gravy is also known to work well as a facial moisturizer, cleaning fluid and spermicide. The woman's jaw dropped — I think she believed me."

My passengers laughed. "My God!" Donna said. "I don't even want to consider the spermicide scenario!"

"If I may ask, what are you ladies doing out so late? Have you been breaking the hearts of the college boys?"

"Oh, yes — that's *exactly* what we've been up to," Donna replied with a chuckle. "Actually Janey and I both have 2-year-olds. Her husband, Bill, dropped us downtown earlier. It's our first night out like this for God knows how long. Certainly since the kids were born — wouldn't you say, Janey?"

"Donna, at this point I can't even remember my life before Sarah came along."

We cruised onto the Interstate and, just before the Taft Corners exit on the north side of the highway, the sculpture of the two Vermont "land" whales came into view, the tail fins of the magnificent beasts glowing in the pale yellow moonlight. I always picture them swimming regally up the Hudson into Lake Champlain, and then upstream in the Winooski River. What possessed them to leap from the water at Exit 12? Was the lure of Wal-Mart just too great?

I thought about the two women softly talking and laughing in the back seat. I knew they were moms the moment they got in the cab. To me, a woman who has had a child is different: her voice, her eyes, the entire way she carries herself. It's like a part of her heart is spliced off and dwells with another person, her kid, and there it remains whether the offspring is 4 or 40. Call it another example of my over-active imagination, but I swear I can see it.

There was a lull in the conversation in the back and I said, "Hey, so tell me — what *did* you guys do downtown on your big night out?"

"Well, first we went to the Pub & Brewery," Donna replied. "They do this thing where you get a sample of all their home brews — like, six of them — in these cute little glasses."

"Yeah," Janey jumped in, "and then we went dancing at Metronome. It was some kind of 'retro' night, kind of like '80s music — but I can't tell for sure anymore. The DJ was amazing though. It was great."

"Janey, that was hilarious when you confronted that young guy who was acting like such a buffoon. What did you say to him, anyway? Afterward, he totally quieted down."

"I told him that if he's trying to appeal to women, that kind of behavior is not going to cut it. I don't know what came over me; I felt like I was his aunt or something."

"Janey, that was *so* you. I loved it!"

"The dancing was a blast, though, wasn't it? It feels great to cut loose like that."

"Yeah," Donna replied. "It was fantastic. We've got to do this more often."

"Fat chance of that," Janey said, and they both laughed.

We got off at the Richmond exit and took the right turn at the town's only traffic light. At the Round Church we swung south onto the Huntington Road. There's been quite a lot of development just south of town, but of course you can say that same thing about every town in Chittenden County. We then turned up into the hills, where the two friends had houses not far from each other.

We stopped first to drop Janey off at her place. As she handed her friend some money to split the fare, the sweetest, most plaintive look come over her face. She took Donna's hands in hers and said, "We're still hotties, aren't we?"

"You bet we are, girl!" Donna said, and gave her friend a big hug. "Hotter than ever."

The Last Ride of Donna Traficante

I pulled over in front of one of the wonderful, rambling Victorians on South Winooski Avenue. Along that stretch south of Spruce, the houses on the east side of the street are built into a steep hill, their front steps angling sharply up from the sidewalk to the entranceways.

Sprawling down the steps from the porch, about a dozen people, all in their late twenties and early thirties, watched me pull to a stop. It was a clear, sunny morning — one of the first truly warm spring days — and most of the group had fished out their shorts and T-shirts for the occasion. A couple of suitcases were sitting on the very top step.

A sweet wind came off the lake, gently fluttering the fresh blossoms of a small dogwood on the front lawn. It was the kind of glorious May day that instantly redeems the relentless winter, whisking clear the gray cobwebs, reminding us why we live here in northern Vermont.

"Donna!" one of the women yelled in the direction of the front screen door. "It's show time! Your taxi's here."

Out the front door emerged Donna Traficante, all five feet of her, slim and sprightly. Her reddish hair was cut in a short shag, and whether or not the color was God-given, the look suited her perfectly. She had a boxy backpack slung over her left shoulder and carried a stuffed canvas bag in her right hand.

"Jernigan," she called down to me, "wouldja come up here and take a group photo? You know — for posterity and all that."

"Hey, it would be an honor, Donna," I replied, and two-stepped up the incline. One of her friends, a lanky guy with bushy blonde hair and a beard, handed me a disposable camera and pointed out the simple controls. Donna dropped her bags and settled into the more-or-less center of the pack.

The affection among this group of friends, and especially towards their departing member, was evident in their physical comfort with each other.

The jostling was gentle as arms draped around shoulders, legs crisscrossed, and the silly banter associated with these occasions carried a real warmth and knowingness. I called out the, "cheese!" and snapped a few shots.

The crew then moved *en masse* down to the taxi. I couldn't carry a thing; her friends all wanted to help. This small gesture of carrying Donna's stuff and loading it into the cab seemed meaningful to them. The good-bye hugs went on for quite a while, with a lot of whispered, last-minute words of encouragement. Tears flowed.

We rode silently towards the airport, the radio off, Donna beside me absorbed in thought. Though she was but a sporadic customer of mine, I was beginning to experience unexpected twinges of sadness over her imminent departure. Donna struck me as a person both serious-minded and playful — an atypical combination of character traits I find tremendously appealing. It dawned on me just how much I'd enjoyed the small amount of time I'd been lucky to spend with her. As we stalled in traffic at the university, she suddenly spoke.

"I can't believe I'm actually doing this," she said, wiping a stray tear from her cheek with the back of her hand. "I left a job I really liked, and I love this town." She paused and gazed out at the college green. A team of UVM maintenance guys wielding mowers, clippers and rakes were fanned out, sprucing things up for the upcoming graduation ceremonies. "What a day to leave. I mean, how gorgeous is this weather?"

"You seem to have a great bunch of friends, and a cool living situation," I said. "Why *are* you giving all this up?"

"I'm coming out of an intense one-year relationship that broke up badly, and I just have to get away. I found a job in Baltimore where my brother lives."

"That's rough," I said, as the traffic began moving again. "You mean it was one of those 'this-town-ain't-big-enough-for-the-two-of-us' deals? You seem to be walking away from a lot over a guy you're not even seeing anymore."

Donna pressed her lips together. "It's more than this guy," she said. "I've been here since I'm 18. I was one of those UVM'ers who graduated and never left. It's been great, but something inside is telling me now's the time to move on. The relationship disaster sort of brought all those feelings to a head."

We took the left off Williston Road at the Ho-Hum Motel, and entered the wide semi-circle in front of the airport terminal.

"Jernigan, tell me this," she said as we came to a halt by the main entrance. Her left elbow was resting on the armrest between our seats, her chin in her palm. She was looking at me with earnest and open eyes. "Did you ever make a major life decision that was really painful, but somehow you just knew you had to do it?"

"Yes, Donna," I replied, "I have indeed."

"Well, how did it turn out?"

"It turned out just fine," I said. "I really don't think you can go wrong following your deepest intuition. Making those lists of pros and cons only gets you so far, if you know what I mean."

Donna chuckled and nodded her head. She paid the fare, and this time I got to help carry her luggage. We plopped everything down at the United ticket counter. Although we didn't know each other real well, she gave me a farewell hug. Like her friends on South Winooski Avenue, I think I needed it.

Winterization

"Go ahead, Carolyn," I joked to a regular customer I had just picked up at her Willard Street apartment. "Blow my mind. Tell me you're meeting your husband at some restaurant other than Sakura."

Carolyn, sitting next to me, broke into a wide smile. She's a handsome, energetic woman — small in stature, but large of heart, and I always look forward to her calls. She turned to face me with warm, dark eyes.

"Then be prepared to have your mind blown," she replied, always a willing partner in my style of fooling around, "'cause tonight we're eating at Smokejacks. I never thought I'd see the day, but Jim said he's finally getting sick of raw fish!"

Carolyn is a much-in-demand nutrition consultant to multinational food manufacturers. Jim, her husband, is a well-respected patent attorney. With two such high-powered careers, I used to wonder why this couple lived in a nice, but relatively modest, second-floor apartment at the south end of Willard Street. Then, in conversation, it came out that they kept the place in Burlington because of its proximity to the airport (both their jobs entailed a lot of air travel), not to mention all the great restaurants. Their main residence, it turned out, was a 4000 square-foot, three-car-garage split-level on an ocean of acreage out in Fairfax.

Passing the noble Union Street Victorians, I glanced at the maple trees set here and there on the front lawns. The foliage season is definitely *kaput*, I thought as I watched the last of the desiccated, umber leaves shiver on stark branches.

"So are you ready for the winter this year?" I asked.

Carolyn and Jim have lived here since the mid-'90s, but I know that Carolyn has never acclimated to the yearly freeze. If you truly dislike cold weather, as I've remarked to more than one would-be emigrant to Vermont, this is not the place to live. An obvious observation, but you'd be surprised how many visitors, enthralled with the verdant mid-summer splendor, fail to consider what it's like here from November to March.

"No, I'm not ready. I'm never ready," Carolyn replied glumly. "I know I've mentioned this to you before, and I keep waffling back and forth, but this might be our last year here. I mean, Jim loves it. He's invigorated by the cold, for chrissake. But me — well, it just wears me down."

I glided to a stop in front of Smokejacks. Jim stood waiting under the awning. He hustled around to my window, wallet in hand.

"Jernigan, my man," he said, as he paid the fare. "Did you hear the big news? I'm weaning off sushi!"

"Yeah," I said. "Carolyn told me. If it gets rough, I believe there's a 12-step program that can help."

"Well, I'm just taking it one day at a time," he said, with a chuckle. "We'll call you later, OK?"

"Sure," I replied. "Just call me when you need me."

Carolyn drifted in and out of my thoughts for the next couple of hours. She wouldn't be the first to pack it in and relocate to more forgiving climes. No doubt, the Vermont winters are long and harsh, and have always functioned as a filter that screens out all comers not entirely committed to making a life in the Green Mountains. The process is not pretty, almost Darwinian, but for those of us who deeply appreciate the spirit of Vermont, the challenging weather is where it all begins. I just wished it wasn't sifting Carolyn.

Just after 11, Jim called for the return trip. They got in the back seat, Carolyn carrying a doggie bag.

"Here you go, Jernigan," she said, passing the bag to me over the front seat. "These appetizers were delicious, so we got you an order. Thought you might enjoy a late-night snack."

"Jesus, guys — that's really sweet. This is a first; none of my customers has ever fed the driver before. Well, yeah, people will pass me the occasional slice of pizza, but you bought this specially for me. I'm touched."

Jim said, "Our pleasure, Jernigan. Hey, we're just in a great mood tonight. Over dinner, Carolyn came to a major decision, and I guess we're feeling celebratory."

"Really?" I said. "What's the big news, if it's OK to ask?"

Carolyn placed both her hands on the top of the seat in front of her, and pulled herself to close to the headrest. She's a small person, as I said, so that took quite a forward movement. She then spoke, sounding full of optimism.

"We're here to stay, Jernigan. I thought about it and realized this has become my home. I like it here too much. Too many things are too good about life in Vermont to leave it all behind because of a few months of cold and ice."

I said, "That's great. Glad to hear it!"

This *was* an encouraging development, and I hoped it was true. Still, I couldn't help but wonder what will happen when Carolyn wakes up, say, the first week of April, to a foot of fresh snow. . .

State of the Reunion

It was the witching hour — 2 a.m. on a Saturday night — and, right on schedule, the downtown bars disgorged their parishioners. As I steered my taxicab down the hill, I could see a couple of dozen of people standing in the street, arms raised in cab-hailing semaphore.

The late-night crowd regularly grouses about the dearth of cabs at closing time. I've given up responding with the simple supply-and-demand explanation: It would be economic suicide for the cab companies to build up their fleets based on the off-the-chart spike in demand that comes and quickly ebbs within one hour of bar closing. All the public knows is, "Where the hell are the cabs?"

I pulled over and two women, perhaps in their early thirties, jumped in the back, while a younger-looking man took the front seat. One of the women, with stylishly-streaked short blonde hair, said, "The Day's Inn, on Route 15, please," and I spun the cab around.

"We're up visiting for our St. Mike's 10th reunion," said the other woman, who, like her friend, was very young-professional looking. "And, I'll tell you, this college life feels like a lifetime ago."

"You got that right, Kristin," the first woman interjected. "Anyway, it isn't the same without the Blarney Stone. Remember our junior year? We, like, lived at that bar."

As we ascended the Main Street hill, the guy next to me blurted out, "Rumsey Lane." I glanced over and took him in for the first time. He appeared, as the Phish song puts it, "foggy, rather groggy."

I turned to the girls in the back. "Isn't he with you?"

"Not really," Kristin coolly replied.

"Never saw him before in my life," said her friend.

"Well then, d'ya mind if I drop him on the way?"

Rumsey Lane is a tiny, unpaved road off Chase Street, right before the Winooski Bridge. It would only be a five-minute detour on the way to the Day's Inn.

"Sure," came the reply from the back. "Go ahead — make some money."

"Hey, man, ya know what?" my seatmate asked.

"No, I don't know what," I replied. "Please tell me."

"It's my friggin' 21st birthday, and I lost my friends downtown."

"Well, that happens," I said. "Ya gotta keep an eye on them."

Not exactly sparkling repartee. I could've just as well been reciting "The Marseillaise." This kid was hammered; we were having only the sketchiest semblance of a conversation.

In slow motion, he pivoted in his seat. "Well, *hello* ladies! Wanna, like, come back to my place?"

"No, I don't think so," Kristin replied, with a curtness designed to forestall any further entreaty.

We made it to Chase Street, and I took the right onto Rumsey, pulling to a stop between the two wood-frame houses which make up the street.

"Dude," the young man said. "D'ya, like, take credit cards?"

"No, I don't. The fare's seven bucks. Can't ya just go in the house, and get some cash from your friends?"

"Oh, I got cash in the apartment, all right. I'll go get it."

He then exited the cab, and walked, in serpentine fashion, like he was evading sniper fire, up to the front steps and into the house.

"Jeez, girls — I'm sorry about this," I said, turning to the face the rear seat.

"Don't worry about it," Kristin said. "It's almost funny, really."

Then, out of nowhere, the taxi was suddenly surrounded by a bunch of young people. They must have emerged from one or both of the houses, but I sure didn't see them coming. In the vapory street light, the effect was very *Night of the Living Dead.* One of the unkempt members of the horde tapped on my window, and I lowered it.

"Dude, did you, like, bring Kevin home? Where'd ya find him? He was, like, totally toasted, and then he, like, disappeared."

I said, "It's his birthday, right? Ya wanna pay his seven dollar cab fare? It could be your own very special birthday gift to him."

"No can do, bro," the friend replied. "How about an E-pill? Would you take a hit of ecstasy for the fare?"

"This isn't happening," Kristin said, to no one in particular.

I looked to my right to see Kevin lurching back to the cab. He opened the front door, and passed me a hundred-dollar bill.

"It's all I got, man. Can ya break it?"

I counted out 93 bucks, and handed it to him. That night, I had been swamped with singles, so I had to give him 38 ones with the change. He stood there listing like he was on a skiff in choppy water, staring blankly at the wad of bills. Finally, he said, "Lemme count it. So's I can give ya a tip."

He then commenced counting — at glacial speed — the stack of money.

"Let's get out of here, please!" Kristin barked. "For the love of God, I'll cover his freaking tip!"

Fully appreciating the suggestion, I threw the transmission into reverse, and backed out of Slackertown, steering a course to the Day's Inn.

"You know," Kristin said, with an audible sigh, as we drove through Winooski, "I think I'd rather keep my college years frozen in time."

"Yeah," I said. "I know just what you mean. The pleasure of nostalgia is the warm, fuzzy glow that grows warmer and fuzzier with each passing year. Who wants reality intruding on the memories?"

Kristin's friend, who had been nearly silent for the whole trip, sat forward in her seat. "This is what I think, Kristin: These reunions are just not all they're cracked up to be."

Something in the Air

"Jernigan, can you come get me?" Wendy, a steady customer, was calling from the restaurant bar where she frequently holds court after she gets off work at the hospital. She's not a big drinker; she just likes to hang out at this classy, friendly place where everybody knows her name.

"My pleasure, Wendy." I replied. "I'll be there in 10."

If I were to take inventory, I suspect I'd find a common thread among many of my regular fares: a revoked driver's license. Hence, their dependence on taxis.

But that's not the case with Wendy. She's an upstanding citizen, albeit one with a peculiar, possibly unhealthy attachment to her vintage Saab. More often than not, she calls me because the Saab is out of commission, parked in the mechanic's shop in one or another stage of disassembly. That's what she claims, anyway, though I have a sneaking suspicion she's just one of those people who prefer not to drive.

Wendy popped out the door just as I pulled up to the curb. This is clearly a woman with her own sense of style, I thought. On this frigid night she wore an oversized black down jacket and a black miniskirt. Though she's hitting middle-age and on her face, pretty as it is, you can trace the lines of a tough life — a bad divorce on top of years of stressful nursing shifts — she still has the slender, graceful legs of a teenage cross-country runner. I like to think of her miniskirts as Wendy's personal gift to the men of Burlington — an unexpected and innervating sight as winter relentlessly marches on.

"Just when you think it can't get any wackier . . ." she said as she closed the door with a whoosh and settled into a comfortable sitting position next to me.

"Tough shift tonight, huh, Wendy?"

"Jernigan, it's not a hospital, it's a lunatic asylum. I just can't figure out who are the guards and who are the inmates. Don't get me started."

I love getting her started and she knows it. Though she tends toward the dramatic, Wendy's humor is ironic and bone-dry. Life has thrown her a succession of curveballs but some core of positive energy has warded off any trace of bitterness. In the battle with the blues, her risibility has been her anodyne.

"So what's going on with the B&B? Is it still a happening thing?"

"We'll see. The zoning issues are unbelievably complex; red-tape up the yin-yang. I'm still working on it, though."

Wendy has a plan to open a bed-and-breakfast in the coastal community of Rockport, Massachusetts. She has some connection to this venerable fishing village through her Portuguese roots. I think she'd make a great innkeeper. Among her many talents, she's a fabulous cook and world-class schmoozer.

The thing is, I don't know if this project will ever move beyond the planning stage. Everyone needs a dream, an interior retreat from the daily grind. Although Wendy contends with an often-maddening job, she's lived in Burlington for many years. With her warm personality and outgoing nature, she's developed a circle of true friends. When you're lucky enough to have a group of people who genuinely care about you, that's a lot to give up.

We cruised down College Street toward the big lake. It's frozen over now — "locked" as the Vermonters say — so all that unearthly steaming has come to an end. It was another one of those artic nights that's been marking this winter as one for the ages. Bearing down on the waterfront with the white moon over the Adirondacks, the dark frozen water looming ahead, and a star-splattered sky above our heads, it felt like a billion degrees below zero. I thought about the strange power of this rarefied air, how it seems to focus the consciousness — clarifying, dissolving the mental dross, expunging the trivial.

We crossed Battery Street, took the right onto Lake and quickly came upon Wendy's home — a three-story, light-gray metal condominium fashioned from an old factory. It's a one-of-a-kind edifice, and given the dearth of available private land in this prime section of town, I doubt we'll soon, if ever again, see an apartment development of this type along the waterfront. Cool people have been drawn to live here and Wendy is one of them.

I swung through the parking lot, pulling as close to the entrance as possible. Above the front door was a sign that read *Arahmi.* I've heard various renderings of its meaning. One resident told me it meant "community." Another defined it as "friends." As chance would have it, one day I drove

Harry Atkinson — the visionary developer of the property — and I put the question to him. He said *Arahmi* was an Abenaki Indian word which translates as "A place that I want to be."

Wendy paid the fare and released the car door to exit. The rush of air was bracing. "Whoa!" she said.

"You got that right," I piped in.

Smiling wryly, she said, "How can I *possibly* leave all this?"

I grinned and said, "That reminds me of something this old guy once told me: 'We'll fight 'til hell freezes over, and then we'll fight on the ice.' I can't recall what it was in reference to, but it rings a bell, doesn't it?"

"Inspirational, Jernigan. Truly."

"Stay warm, Wendy," I said, chuckling at her deadpan demeanor.

"You too," she responded. Then she turned and scurried up to the beckoning door of *Arahmi.*

4

PRIDE AND PREJUDICE

Conventional wisdom holds that we in Vermont are a tolerant bunch. Live and let live is the prevailing social ethos. And, when it comes to challenging oppression, Vermont has a lot to be proud of as the first state to outlaw slavery, and the first to legislate full legal benefits for same-sex couples.

But before we get too self-congratulatory, it's noteworthy that Vermont has historically been one of the whitest states in the nation, to the tune of 98-99%. Therefore, in reality, our good intentions have been mostly theoretical.

Recently, however, many more minorities have begun to settle in the state, including significant numbers of immigrants from Africa and Southeast Asia. So, now perhaps the open heart of the Green Mountains will be put to the test.

Lemongrass and Maple Syrup

A few nights a week in the Queen City's geographical and spiritual center — Nectar's Restaurant and Lounge — a tiny Tibetan man serves up the hot, open turkey sandwiches and french fries.

"Make it a large," I call to him through the sliding, street-level takeout window. Above my head, the town's sole rotating neon sign (grandfathered-in years ago with the then-new signage regulations) beams out "Nectar's" in glowing orange script. The sidewalk is jammed with people as a pumping disco bass line reverberates in the air — it's '70s night upstairs at Club Metronome. "Sure, right away," he says. "You want gravy, no-gravy?"

"Hold the gravy, OK? But douse those babies in catsup, willya?"

With a practiced flourish, the small man bangs the fry basket three times against the side of the fryolator, and flips a cascade of french fries into the waiting clamshell box he has balanced in his left hand. He then places the white box on the cutting board and grabs not one, but two red, plastic cylinders. Two-gun style, he paints those taters red, snaps the box closed and passes it to me through the window.

"Here you go. Plenty catsup. Four dollar, please."

He seems genuinely happy to be there, a fry cook in the bustle of downtown Burlington. I don't know what I more enjoy — the Nectar's fries or our short exchange.

A few hundred Vietnamese, Cambodians, Chinese and Tibetans now call Vermont their home. They live throughout Chittenden county, but mostly in apartments in Winooski and the Burlington's Old North End. For those of us who've lived here for years, the winters are long and frigid. One can only imagine what the first winter feels like to people who have grown up in the jungle climate of Southeast Asia. But, just as it's always been for American immigrants, things are better for them here, often immeasurably so. They'll gladly tolerate the Vermont winters; it's a small price to pay.

Last July, I remember clearing (cab-speak for dropping a fare) in Winooski at dusk on a warm summer day. In the fading pink and purple streams of light, I saw a half-dozen Vietnamese men sitting along the curb on West Allen Street. (I *think* they were Vietnamese; in the finest tradition of American cultural ignorance, I have difficulty distinguishing among people of various Asian backgrounds.) They were smoking cigarettes and laughing; they looked relaxed and happy. Across the street, children ran in the small playground. I couldn't say if they were melting in a pot, but it was wonderful to see Asian, black and white kids yelling and playing together. I remember thinking, *this bodes well for our community if we adults don't screw it up.*

Mr. Chang always arrives on the late bus from New York City. He carries a frayed, green valise in one hand, and a medium-sized, white garbage bag stuffed to the gills in the other. The plastic bag contains fish, or some manner of sea life. I know this because I asked him about the smell the first time he took my taxi. "This is for restaurant," he told me. "I cook there." I'd say the fish (or whatever) is deceased, but I wouldn't swear to it. In any event, it's a lively, squishy package he places down on the front car mat between his feet. For the remainder of the evening, the car always smells, wondrously, of the ocean.

Yesterday I had the pleasure — some part of me wants to say honor — of driving a recently-arrived immigrant couple. As soon as they entered the cab, I guessed they were from Tibet. Both the man and woman wore similar coats of thick fabric, perhaps cotton batting. The garments were colorful, but of a soft, muted quality. Maybe it's another of my gringo stereotypes, but the Tibetan people seem to be quite short, as were these folks. They both had black hair and broad, handsome faces. Another thing is, they were quiet. Not dreamy, as in reverie, but self-contained, awake, alive. I have always been drawn to people with such a peaceful presence, undoubtedly because my own energy spills out of me like some leaky, dyspeptic garden hose.

Rolling along Hyde Street, I couldn't (of course) help myself. "Tell me," I said. "Did you folks ever meet the Dalai Lama?"

"We have been with His Holiness in India," the man said. "How do *you* know the Dalai Lama?"

"Jeez, everyone knows the Dalai Lama," I replied. "I think he's even visited Vermont a couple times."

The man smiled sweetly and said, "What do *you* think of the Dalai Lama?"

Oh, baby. The Dalai Lama is the physical embodiment of Tibetan culture, national aspiration and spirituality — like Mahatma Gandhi, George Washington and Mother Teresa rolled into one. *Please,* I uttered to myself, *don't say something sickeningly trite to these people.*

"I think he's beautiful," I said. I had not a clue where that came from, but not too shabby, I thought, considering the full-fledged brain lock that had taken hold.

"Yes," the woman said. "He *is* beautiful."

The Burlington to which I migrated over 25 years ago is different from the Burlington of this moment. When I got off the boat that summer of '79, the town boasted five, count 'em five, pizza places. The current phone book lists 47. The population back then was almost entirely white. Now along with the influx of Asians, many Africans and African-Americans, Eastern Europeans, and even a smattering of Hispanic folks have put down roots in the Queen City.

Change is hard for me. If I return home to find the couch moved to the other side of the room, this throws me off for a week. But if I open my heart and mind to simply experience the new crop of people who work, shop and live here, and who now ride in my taxi, the feeling is, well, beautiful.

The Shape of the Bottle

When you see them on the street, you think you know, but you don't. The fallacy continues even as they hail you and enter the cab. I'm speaking of humans, and my endless proclivity to believe I can divine a person's character based on what he or she looks like. You'd think after being proven wrong, often dead wrong, for the 11,000th time, I'd give it a rest. But like the similarly misplaced faith I place in movie reviews, meteorological forecasts and book covers, I just can't shake the habit.

I slowed down at the sight of a massive, waving arm in front of Ri-Ra, the downtown "Irish" pub. (I use quotation marks, because I'm naturally suspicious of the strident use of any type of "authenticity" as a marketing tool. On the other hand, during the renovation process the place was indeed rife with honest-to-goodness, true-blue or, I guess that would be, true-green, Irishmen.)

"Mate, mate! Yeah, you. Will you take us to Tracy Drive, then?"

The speaker and his two mates were big, burly and boisterous; they were barrel-chested, barrel-legged and, I kid you not, barrel-headed. If they got the notion, it struck me, it would not be out of the question for the three of them to lift up my taxi and carry it to Tracy Drive, perhaps at an easy jog.

"I'll take you anyplace in the continental U.S. or Canada," I replied. "Jump in."

Into the cab they advanced. One guy, the most jumbo of the jumbos, got in next to me, and the cab-hailer along with the third man sat in the rear. I took a moment to appreciate the car technology that has brought us struts, shocks and springs. Taking them for Australians in light of the "mate" stuff, I asked, "So, what brings you Aussies to town?"

"Those two bozos in the back, they're Aussies, man. I come from South Africa. All of us, we're in rugby club."

Wow, South Africa, I thought. Visitors from that country are far and few between. A favorite aspect of my job is interacting with foreigners, and now I had another pin for my map.

The South African appeared to be in his late-twenties, which means he'd lived through, experienced first-hand, a cultural and political sea change: the dismantling of apartheid. My immediate impulse was to ask him about that journey — what was it like? But I stopped myself.

I looked at his skin-tight. sleeveless T-shirt, his buzz-cut blonde hair, and I "knew" he was a racist. There's no way to discuss the tragic history of South Africa without consideration of race, and I was in no mood to deal with, that is, confront, a prejudiced opinion. But you know me.

"The ending of apartheid," I said, "and the dropping of the international boycott must have made things a heckuva lot better for you South African athletes."

"Oh, you're not kidding," he replied. "We can play all over the world now. It's friggin' marvelous."

"What was it like when it was going down? You must have been a teenager."

The South African shifted in his seat. The bluster of the young-man-out-on-the-town evaporated from his cheeks and eyes, replaced by a pensive expression. I noticed his teammates in the back had grown quiet as well. There was only the humming of the engine and the whirring of the tires on the Northern Connector.

"I can't describe what is has meant for my country," he said. "It's the most wonderful thing. Now we are really one country. Nelson Mandela — what he's done for us, it's friggin' awesome. I'm talking about all of us, not just the black people."

With his Afrikaner accent, black became *bleck*. Just hearing that sound, you expect bigoted dogma. But there I was learning, for Time #11,001, that the shape of the bottle has nothing to do with the taste of the wine.

Heartened and encouraged, I continued, "What was it like for your parents; how did they respond to the change?"

"My father believes, to this day, that blacks are biologically inferior to white people. This is what he would tell us all through our childhood." He was squinting as he spoke, as if it was painful for him to recount this to me. "Then, of course, for all the holidays he would invite Mbuso, the family gardener — we have a good-sized parcel of land — well, he'd invite him to have meals with us. He would treat Mbuso with the utmost respect, even affection. So, the whole thing is complex."

"Is it an open conflict when you and your dad talk about this stuff?" I asked.

"No, not at all. This is what he told me: 'Alec, I'm old; I'm set in my ways; I can't change — it's too late for me. You go form your own opinion. Be your own man. I will respect that.'"

"That's amazing," I said, "that your dad could hold such a close-minded view of his fellow man, and yet maintain, as a father, such an open-minded relationship with you."

"That's my dad," he said with a laugh. "He's a strange one."

Later that night, during the lull preceding last call, I sat at a taxi stand and mulled over this fare. I thought about how I keep struggling to pin down this world, to explain the nature of people to myself in some reliable way. I want a large, muscle-bound, tattooed young man to be a small-minded oaf, not a big-hearted, contemplative person. I want racist, Afrikaner farmers to be oppressive and controlling as fathers, not fair-minded and supportive. I want people to behave in conformity with my preconceptions — to quit surprising me and upsetting my carefully-constructed world.

I'm not that old, I thought to myself, *not that set in my ways.* Maybe it's not too late for me to bring some mindfulness to my interaction with others: to discover others in the living reality of the moment rather than dwell in the frozen, jaundiced and lifeless world of prejudgment.

"The Best Western, please." A bouffant blonde in tight, black Capri pants was standing at my taxi window. *Well,* I thought, *I know where* she's *at.*

Jeez, I guess I still have some work to do.

Another Day at the Office

Coming off the bus, the woman was struggling with two bulky pieces of luggage. She gave me a pointed forefinger wave, signaling she wanted my cab, and began walking towards me.

"Let me help you with those," I said, moving quickly to meet her.

"Why, thank you," she said. "That's very sweet of you. They weigh a ton."

"No problem." I swung the bags into the trunk and we were off.

"You look like it's been a long journey," I said, just some polite cabbie small talk offered to the weary-looking woman now sitting in the rear seat.

"Oh, I guess maybe," she replied. "I left Sarasota yesterday morning. It was horrible, all the way up to D.C. I kid you not — I was the only white person on the bus!"

I hate that stuff. I really do. A few years ago, I would have come down on the speaker like a sledgehammer. But inevitably, post-confrontation, I would find myself gagging on the aftertaste of holier-than-thou. So, I let it pass.

Turning north onto South Union Street, we passed the row of gorgeous Victorians which sit up and back from the street.

"I used to live there when I was a kid," she said, pointing out one of the stately buildings.

"Is that so?" I said.

"Yeah, my aunt married a guy named Rabin who owned the property. When I was in second or third grade, my mother and I went to live with them."

"You must have some fond memories," I offered.

"Not really," she replied. "He kicked us out when I was 12. He was a Jew, you know."

Click. "OK, so let me sort this out," I said. "You don't like blacks and you don't like Jews. Any other groups of people you wanna add to this list?"

"What are you talking about?" she shot back, her voice rising in indignation. "Who said I don't like Jews?"

"All right," I counter, and now I was off and running. "What about the crack about the bus ride?"

"What about the bus ride? Exactly how does that prove I hate blacks?"

Against all odds, I managed to shut up. This discussion was the opposite of enlivening. I mean, what was I arguing about?

My self-imposed silence lasted — no surprise — about one minute.

"Let's say I'm an African-American," I began again, once more into the breach. "Do you still tell me about this horrible bus ride with all those black people?"

"Sure, why not?" she replied. "That's the big problem these days. Everybody has to be so politically correct."

OK, I get it. It's not racial intolerance that's tearing apart our country, our world. It's the inability to spout bigotry free from the inconvenient annoyance of public condemnation. *That's* the big problem. Thank goodness someone invented the phrase "politically correct," so we now have an effective talisman, a potent inoculation against such damaging invective.

I'm beginning to lose it — "it" being the reflective sense of self that exists beyond the whirlpool of passionate feelings. It's a fine line between righteous and self-righteous. You cross it when you're convinced of your moral superiority over another. But, more than that, here was the clinker, the ultimate irony in what had become a dismal conversation: At this point, I hated this woman, and that's most dispiriting of all.

I thought of the brilliance of Martin Luther King. He had it figured out: hate cannot transform hate; love, or at least open-heartedness, is the only thing that holds the possibility of changing another; non-violence can transform anger. In my mind, I flashed on the famous *Life* magazine photo of the black students sitting on counter stools at a "white's only" luncheonette. A gang of white people surround them, their mouths open in obvious taunts and laughter. One of the white men has just emptied a milk shake over the head of one of the male students. The image has always stuck in my mind — the blazing courage of those students in their refusal to meet that violence with violence in return. What power.

"You know what?" I said as we pulled up to her house. "I apologize for coming off like I'm criticizing you as a person. It's just that I think people are all the same, at least in the ways that really matter. Everybody's just tryin'a get by, tryin'a find some connection, some kinda love in this harsh world. (When I get upset, the New York accent of my youth seems to re-emerge in its full-bodied state.) Doncha think it helps if we all try to treat each other with respect?"

Not exactly super-articulate, but at least I was back to seeing her as a fellow human being — just one of the tribe who happens to be walking around with some misdirected anger. I can empathize because I too have that problem. In my case, it manifests in different ways, at different targets, but it's the same core problem.

I removed her luggage from the trunk and carried it up to the porch of her home. She took out the fare, included a tip, and handed it to me. She looked me in the eye and said, "Thanks." I looked back and said, "Well, thank you."

Maybe I'm kidding myself, but now in middle age this is what I've come to believe: every exchange with another matters. There's a hidden purpose behind the movement of people in and out of our lives, even the so-called "strangers."

As I pulled away from the curb, I felt shaken from the discordant exchange, yet appreciative of this woman. She revealed to me something of my own intolerance. It's painful to see parts of yourself you would rather ignore, but in my experience, discomfort is the price tag of any meaningful personal growth. At these moments of self-revelation, my resistance is a mountain, and my immediate reaction is to whine, complain and rationalize. Deep down, though, I know it's worth the price.

Manual Tranny

"I've got four here at Pearl's goin'a Winooski. How long they wanna know."

It was a bartender calling on a frigid night. Pearl's is a bar located on Pearl Street, what a coincidence. It used to be Burlington's "gay" bar, and a lot of locals still think of it that way. But either it's changed or we've changed, because it's now the "all-sexual-orientations-welcome" bar. This conclusion, by the way, is based solely on observation of my cab fares going to the place. I've never set foot in Pearl's nor, for that matter, most of the other Burlington bars. I drive bar-hoppers all night long but I'm not one in civilian life. Ironic, isn't it?

"Tell 'em 10 minutes," I replied.

Approaching the bar, I saw two women and two men on the sidewalk doing the wind-chill shuffle. Even before I came to a full stop, they were grabbing at the door handles. One of the women, tall and big-boned, plopped down with a thud into the shotgun seat and said, "Mr. Cabbie, you are my knight in shining armor. You've rescued me from this cruel cryogenic experiment."

The folks in the back laughed heartily. "Tyler," the other woman said, "you come up to visit us in January and this is what you get. This is Vermont, OK? Now quit the whining, girl."

Tyler reached over and grasped my right forearm. Her fingers were large with candy-apple nails. "Hon," she said, "don't pay no mind to my friends in the back. They're a jealous bunch, these Vermonters."

We were still in park, idling in front of Pearl's. Tyler was looking right at me, a mischievous gleam in her eyes. Her eyelashes, I noticed, were long and fluffy, her cheeks dusted with diamond glitter. I felt myself becoming slightly hypnotized. Tyler must have sensed this, because all of sudden she winked, snapping me out of it.

"Ya know where I'm from, doll?" she asked in a husky growl. "Miami, F.L.A. That's right — we got it goin' on in South Beach!" She lifted her hands up to shoulder level and executed a compact bump-and-grind routine. "The only ice down my way, child, is crushed up in the margaritas!"

"Not to change the subject, but where am I taking you folks?"

"We're at the Woolen Mill," one of the men jumped in from behind me. "And if you could, let's stop at Cumberland Farms on Riverside. We're out of cigarettes."

On the ride to Riverside Avenue, Tyler, a woman who clearly relished the spotlight, held center stage. In the manner of a wayward cheerleader — equal parts perky and profane — she kept us, her audience, fully engaged in the performance. Taking it in, enjoying it really, it struck me that there was something old-fashioned about her distaff sense of humor. The word that popped to mind was "brassy."

"Tyler, it's Parliaments, right?" one of the men asked as we eased to a stop at the convenience store. "Stay here with the cabbie; we'll pick you up a couple packs."

The back seat emptied, and it was me and Tyler. I took a good look at this compelling person. She was an attractive woman, if you could get past the intimidating stature.

"What about you?" she asked. "How long have you lived at the North Pole?"

I smiled and said, "I guess I've been in B-town over 25 years now."

"Well, you're a lucky man. The weather is a bit much for me — I guess that's obvious — but the people are lovely."

Tyler turned her head and, with a long fingernail, scraped a small circle in her frosted window. She glanced out for a moment at the foggy window of the store. It looked cozy in there on this icy night. The bleary, pastel beer signs washed the parking lot in warm hues. She then turned back to face me and gently touched my arm for the second time.

She said, "There's something special about this town. I could sense it bar-hopping with my friends tonight."

Her eyes widened, and it felt like she was letting me in on a secret. With her good looks and irrepressible humor, it was a masquerade that was hers to keep or reveal.

"Well, I'm waiting. " I said. "What exactly is 'so special' about this town?"

"You Burlington folks," she continued, "are open-minded." As she spoke I noticed a slight movement at the throat of her cotton turtleneck.

"Yup, we're an open-minded bunch, all right," I said, and just then her friends came out of the store and scurried back to the taxi. As they piled in and the laughter and chatter started up again, I thought to myself, *My goodness, this is the like* The Crying Game, *but without the tears.*

Flaming Out

I was driving two big guys to a house in Mallet's Bay. Apparently they had been downtown on the prowl for women and had struck out. They were disappointed and expressed it with anger — the one emotion so many men in our culture give themselves permission to display. Not, thankfully, smash-the-taxi-window angry; just peeved-and-ornery angry.

We were driving past a downtown bar when my seatmate turned to his buddy in the back and said, "Randy, you know, I went to school with the guy who owns that place."

"You're kidding, Tommy." Randy replied. "That guy is a big, fat faggot — a real flamer."

"Tell me about it. The funny thing is, his family owns that auto supply place, and they're all normal."

We turned onto North Champlain Street, *en route* to the Northern Connector. I just listened to their conversation. I hate this kind of dull, casual prejudice. Sometimes I say something; usually I don't — unless the customer tries to enlist me in it.

Tommy did, suddenly speaking to me. "*What*, man? You must think something about what we're talking about."

"You really want to know?" I asked.

"Well, yeah."

"I, myself, am completely disinterested what another man does with his penis, so long as he isn't hurting anybody. I mean, Christ, don't we have more important things to worry about in this world than that?"

"Sure, OK," Tommy said. "I don't have any trouble with gays. It's just the flamers. They should be sent away to some island somewhere. They make me *sick*. Do you see what I'm saying?"

"Look," I continued. "I got something to say about that, too, but you ain't gonna like it."

"No, no — go ahead, man. I want to hear it."

"I look at it like this: If you're secure with who you are, being a heterosexual and all that, why should it bother you even one bit if some other guy wants to dress up and act all girly-girly. I mean, who *cares*?"

"Sure — yeah, *riiiight*," Tommy came back. "*That's it* — I'm 'insecure' in my sexuality. Maybe I just can't stomach flamers. Didja ever think it could be as simple as that?"

"I don't know what it is for you, man," I conceded. "I truly don't."

I've been in conversations like this before, and this seemed like the right stop to get off the train. At a certain point, these debates are not about logic or reason, so why bother? Still, there was something in this guy's attitude — a part of him seemed cognizant of how wrong he was, even as he continued spewing garbage.

OK," I ventured ahead. "You wanna try this one on for size? This is the thing about these men you're calling 'flamers.' You know how sometimes acting like a 'man' can be a pain in the ass? Like being tough and macho all the time gets a little tiring? Well, these 'flamers,' like, couldn't care less! I mean — God bless 'em — they've totally opted out of the whole 'manly' game. Ain't it refreshing, in a way?"

"What the *friggin'* hell are you talkin' about, man?" Randy, in the back, who I assumed was tuned out of the conversation, apparently had been listening quite intently. And he didn't like what he was hearing.

"One of these guys comes on to me," he continued, "I'll kick his freakin' ass so fast, I'll knock out him *and* his family!"

"Well, that's something *else*," I replied. I was in too deep to get out now. "We're not talkin' about anybody hitting on anybody."

"Don't listen to Randy," Tommy interjected. "Believe me when I tell ya, he's a bigger moron than me."

"Oh yeah?" Randy shot back. "Well, I might be, like, a bigger moron than you, but you're a bigger faggot than me!"

Oh, this guy's brilliant, I thought. He's like the mother who, in the heat of an argument, calls her offspring a "son-of-a-bitch."

We were nearing the end of the Connector, crossing the wide Heineberg Bridge into Colchester. *This has been one dopey discussion*, I noted to myself, though not a heck of a lot different from so many of these late-night taxi palavers.

We turned right onto Tommy's street, coming to a stop in front of his family's home. Apparently Randy was staying overnight; there was some talk of Spaghettios and ESPN-2. We pulled up to the house, and Tommy turned to me as he fished out the money for the fare.

"I want you to know something," he said. "I'm the only one in my family who thinks this way. They're all, like, real liberal and everything. They can't understand how I believe this stuff. So don't hold it against them."

This was too much for me to hold my tongue. This whole thing, keep in mind, had started with a conversation about "normal" families and their supposed black sheep.

"Let me get this right, man," I said. "You're worried that your intolerant attitude might reflect badly on your family. Did you ever consider that this "flamer" guy who got you so in such a tizzy, well, his family might be completely accepting and even proud of him?"

"Jeez," Tommy replied. "That's kinda ironic."

"Yeah," I said. "Kinda."

Wedding Belles

The two women I picked up at the airport on a recent clear, cold afternoon carried identical forest-green suitcases. One of the women was slender, with her hair piled high in an intricate arrangement and held in place by a pale ivory comb. Her friend was taller, stockier and wore a black leather duster. Both were African-American. They seemed happy to be in Burlington, Vermont; their smiles never ebbed as they settled into the back seat and we got underway.

"You said the Inn at Essex — was that right?" I asked.

"Uh-huh," the shorter woman replied. "It looked like a beautiful place on the Internet. Is it really that nice?"

"Oh yeah, it's a great place, all right. The hotel restaurant is run by a culinary school, so that's an added bonus. Nothing beats a meal prepared and served by people getting graded on their performance."

"Sounds *perfect*," the taller woman said as she reached down and squeezed the hand of her companion. In the rear-view mirror I could see them gazing at each other and beaming.

We cruised up Airport Parkway and came upon the Lime Kiln Bridge, a thin arc high above the Winooski River. An old-timer once told me that, because of its elevation, it was the sole bridge between Lake Champlain and Montpelier to survive the Great Flood of 1927. I miss seeing the ruins of the old lime works. It was leveled last year so the space could be used as a landfill dumpsite for the massive Fletcher Allen excavation. The older I get, the more I appreciate a good ruin. It takes one to know one, I guess.

"Is it always this cold up here?" the taller woman asked as we passed St. Michael's College. "When we booked the weekend, the Chamber of Commerce website said it's usually around 40 degrees this time of year."

"Nope — the website was accurate. This winter's been unusually cold."

"What do *we* know?" the shorter woman said with a laugh. "We're Southern girls!"

"Is that right? What town?"

"The big town — Atlanta, GA."

"Atlanta, huh?" I said, "Just thinking about it warms me up. I visited Stone Mountain one spring about 20 years ago. It was gorgeous — peach blossoms, the whole bit. What brings you folks to Yankee country?"

"Oh, we're up here for a wedding."

"That's always fun. Is it taking place at the Inn? They do a lot of weddings there, you know — the facilities are lovely."

"Yes, the wedding's at the Inn."

"It'll be great," I said. "Yeah, I know something like half the marriages end in divorce, but you gotta be an optimist, right?"

"Yes, I agree. You have to hope and dream."

We turned onto Susie Wilson *en route* to the Circ Highway and the Lang Farm. I know it's now known as the Essex Outlet Center, but I persist in calling it the Lang Farm, as if doing so might make the cows rematerialize where Canadians now forage for Polo designer jeans and discounted Brooks Brothers boxer shorts. What did Vermonters once say with pride? "More cows than people." Now it's more cows on T-shirts than people. *Or* cows.

The two women chatted softly in the back as we made our way along the Circ. Soon the stores came into view and, beyond them, the triangular rooftops of the set of buildings comprising the Inn at Essex.

"There's the hotel," I pointed out to my passengers as we swung off the highway. "So, who's getting married?" I continued, my inveterate nosiness kicking in. "A good friend? A relative?"

There was no response. I glanced at the rear-view and I could see the women were looking at one another again, as if they were communicating telepathically. Then the taller woman said, "We are."

"That's great! Just great," I exclaimed, probably too quickly and eagerly by half.

My comfort level with homosexual people and their romantic relationships is akin to my ability with computers: Openly gay relationships and computer technology were not part of the experience of my formative years. I've since learned about both, but I don't know if I'll ever be a "natural" with either.

We pulled up to the entrance of the Inn and the taller woman paid the fare while her partner lifted out their bags and walked into the front desk.

"Congratulations," I said, "and enjoy your stay in Vermont. I think you'll find the folks up here pretty open-minded."

"So we've been told," she said, still with that warm southern smile — and generously ignoring, I thought, my slight case of foot-in-mouth disease.

Before UV Was Groovy

I stood at the arrival gate on a recent weekday afternoon with a sign reading, "Dr. Rainville." The previous day the good doctor had booked me to transport him to a B&B in Underhill.

As a cabbie, you really want to rendezvous with your fare as he or she comes through the gate. Any airport — even our relatively small-scale Burlington International — is a chaotic place. If you miss your party as they arrive, there's every possibility of never hooking up, even if you have them paged a couple of times.

Coming through the doors, a compact, husky man caught my eye and nodded. He had a precisely-trimmed salt-and-pepper beard outlining a rosy smile.

"You must be Dr. Rainville," I greeted him, extending my hand.

"And you must be Mr. Pontiac," he responded as we shook hands. "Thanks for being on time."

"Please, it's Jernigan," I said, "and 'being-on-time' is my middle name." As that bit of banter left my mouth, I realized how ungainly it sounded. "That doesn't make much sense, does it?"

"No, not too much," the doctor replied, chuckling, "but I get the idea."

"Got any luggage to pick up?" I asked, getting back to business.

"Yes, one bag," he replied, and we made our way over to the baggage belt.

The warning buzzer blared and the luggage parade began. "Up here for the foliage, Doc?" I asked as we watched for his item.

"Not specifically, but I do hope to take in some of the fall sights. Man, oh man, it's been a long time, and I'm enjoying it already. This weekend is my 50th UVM reunion; that's what brings me to Vermont. Hey — there it is."

He yanked a blue suitcase off the belt, and took me up on my offer to be the sherpa. My rule of thumb: If a guy is my age or older, I'll offer to tote the heavier bag. They almost all have wheels now, as did the doctor's — thank goodness.

My taxi was a short walk away in the service lane. Dr. Rainville took the front seat, and we were off. "Fifty years, that's something" I said. "What was UVM like in the '50s?"

"Another world," he replied without hesitation. "For one thing, it was a much smaller school — maybe a couple of thousand students and just a few dorms."

"Were there many female students? What were they called back then — coeds?"

"There were some. They lived in that old dorm on Redstone Campus — Coolidge Hall, I think it was. Their lives were subject to all kinds of restrictions. I remember they had to wear skirts or dresses — they couldn't wear slacks unless the temperature fell below 15 degrees. And then, they had a 10 o'clock curfew, which I think went to midnight on weekends. I remember us guys would get together after the girls' curfew at some diner downtown."

"Would that have been Henry's?" I asked.

"Yes, that's the one. Is it still in business?"

"It sure is. Most of the old places are gone, but Henry's has hung in there."

We passed St. Mike's, the old Fanny Allen and the Fort. The semi-completed Circumferential Highway beckoned. When it comes to the ongoing controversy over this road, my parochial self-interest as a cab driver trumps my concern about urban sprawl. I say, damn the torpedoes and finish the darn thing!

"These colors are outstanding," the doctor said, gazing out at the passing maples. "It's like fruit cocktail."

"That's great, Doc. I thought I'd heard the fall colors compared to just about everything, but 'fruit cocktail' — that's original."

"This time of year reminds of the homecoming incident — I think it was my senior year. Do you know about this?"

"No, but I'm all ears."

"A bunch of us fraternity brothers invited our girlfriends up for the weekend — back then, of course, homecoming centered around the big football game — and we rented a couple of hotel rooms for them. Now, it so happens the president of our frat was a black guy."

"Really?" I jumped in. "That's amazing for the early '50s. How many black students were on campus?"

"Just a handful, maybe four or five, but one of them was our president. Anyway, the hotel owner refused to allow this guy's black girlfriend to stay at the hotel. We weren't going to put up with that, so we organized a demonstration at the Statehouse. Well, the legislature then passed a law forbidding that kind of discrimination in public accommodations. Keep in mind, this was well before the federal Civil Rights Acts of the mid-'60s."

"I didn't know that slice of state history. It speaks well for both UVM and Vermont."

"Thinking back, though, I feel badly about Kake Walk. Do you know about that, Jernigan? It was the single biggest event of the semester, a competition among the frats."

"Yeah, I do. The students dressed in black face and performed, was that it?"

"Yes, it was a talent show, really, with other acts as well. I recall it was held at Memorial Auditorium. Our frat president always said it didn't bother him, but looking back now, I see how that likely wasn't his true feelings. It was probably another of the many injustices he had to live with to get by and succeed in society as it was at the time."

"I can see what you mean," I said, as we negotiated the sharp inclined turn on Route 15 passing through Jericho.

"I do hope he's up for the weekend. I feel like I'd want to apologize to him — 50 years late, but just the same."

"I bet it would mean a lot to him." I said.

We found the B&B, and I again helped him with his bag. Sun-flecked cerise and amber leaves blanketed the front lawn as we walked together to the door. This was Vermont in all its soft splendor.

At the entrance to the inn, the doctor took out his wallet and paid me the fare. I said, "Well, I guess it's not quite a true homecoming weekend without the big football game."

"Football game or not," he replied, "it feels like homecoming to me."

The Two Billion Club

"This is one beautiful state," my passenger said, gazing through the window at the passing meadow. To the east, the Killington mountain peaks still glistened with snow against the blue sky. "I have a buddy back in Baltimore who used to come up here to ski when he was a kid."

We were passing through Pittsford *en route* to Brookside Ranch, a residential psychiatric facility in Cuttingsville, about 15 miles southeast of Rutland. I had learned that my fare was an administrator for a mental health organization based in Washington, D.C. He'd come up to Vermont to evaluate Brookside as a possible treatment option for one of his clients.

Aaron looked about 30, with dark brown skin and keen brown eyes. He was dressed in a cream-colored turtleneck and light suede jacket. Though casual, his entire raiment was polished. Is it just me, or do out-of-staters seem to dress better than Vermonters? Perhaps my perception is skewed, because the visitors I tend to transport are mostly tourists and professional people.

One detail contrasted sharply with Aaron's young-professional presentation: his hair. He had thick dreadlocks tumbling over his shoulders and reaching the center of his back. It wasn't the funky, frizzy affair you might see on a hippie-type; his was clearly a well-groomed coif. Still, it wasn't the look you would expect on a young African-American man rising in his field.

We reached the Brookside Ranch a mile up a dirt road off Route 103. Aaron — who'd done the research prior to taking the trip — told me the place had been in operation as a mental health facility for 70 years, and the "campus" looked like it had expanded building by building over time.

An extensive sugaring operation was also in full swing — the surrounding woods were replete with tapped and tin-bucketed maple trees. A number of people were walking about the property; I couldn't tell who were staff and who were clients. I don't know what I expected: Nurse Ratched and bug-eyed, hysterical people in straitjackets?

We pulled into a parking area adjacent to a building marked, "Office," and Aaron got out to investigate. The parking spots overlooked a fast-flowing stream, which was swollen and bubbling with winter snowmelt. I lowered my window, eased the seat back and closed my eyes to listen to the watery symphony. An hour later, I awoke to Aaron tapping on the windshield.

"Sorry to wake you," he said with a laugh. "You looked like you were into some sweet dreaming."

"No problem, man," I said, shaking off the grogginess. "I actually feel kind of invigorated. Are you all set for the ride back to the airport? Did you accomplish what you needed to?"

"That's 'yes' and 'yes.' I'm quite impressed with this place. It's really a working farm — of sorts, anyway — and they integrate that into the therapy experience."

"Great," I said, "then let's roll."

"Hey, is there a place where we could stop to pick up some Vermont maple syrup? I had some for the first time with waffles this morning at the hotel in Burlington, and I think I'm addicted. I'd like to buy some for gifts."

"Yeah, I know just the place. It's where I get my syrup, too."

About an hour later, we reached Dakin Farm in Ferrisurgh. I love this place, and I stop here every excuse I get. The truth is, the delectable samples they put out — preserves, cheese, ham, crackers — beckon to me every time I'm cruising down Route 7.

The store was crowded with tourists, and the old proprietor himself, Sam Cutting, was scurrying to and fro, cleaning up, replenishing the samples, and talking sugaring with all comers. I stood to the side, downing smoked cheddar cheese cubes and watching as Aaron made his way through the store. He looked like a kid in Disney World, checking out everything from the chutneys to the Vermont T-shirts, all the while talking with the staff and fellow shoppers. People seemed to light up and spontaneously engage with him, so inviting was his presence.

Eventually, I coaxed Aaron out of the store. He had a bag filled with maple syrup, maple powder, maple cream — you name it. *Another Vermont convert*, I thought, as we got underway again.

I kept glancing at the guy's hair as we continued north to the airport. There was something magnificent, almost regal, about it.

"Aaron, if you don't mind my asking, how long did it take you to get the dreadlocks looking that good?"

"Why thanks, man," he replied. "They do tend to shake up some folks. My stepdad, for one, has no idea what it's about." He shook his head and smiled. "To answer your question, I can tell you exactly: I began growing them in 1995, right after the Million Man March."

"Oh, yeah, I remember that — when all those black men assembled in Washington. Did you attend?"

"I did, and it changed my life. It was such an awesomely positive experience. When I got back to Baltimore, I started expressing myself differently, or perhaps I should say more fully. The dreadlocks, I guess, were a physical sign of that change."

"That's deep," I said.

"That it is," he agreed, with a chuckle. "That it is."

I dropped Aaron at Burlington International, and later that night I found myself thinking about him. What impressed me was the guy's authenticity, his willingness to truly be himself.

I used to think that kind of self expression was risky because — heavens! — some people might not like you. But then a friend put it in perspective for me: No matter how you cut it, a third of the people in the world are bound to dislike you, a third will be indifferent, and a third will truly dig you. Why bother, then, to cater to the first two-thirds? The world currently has about six billion inhabitants; that leaves two billion people who'd be happy to meet any one of us.

You can count me squarely among Aaron's two billion.

5

PIQUANT PEOPLE

A lifetime of hacking has provided me vast opportunity for human interaction. And, in my experience, every single person is a walking epic novel. I've grown to truly enjoy the humans, in all their foibles and eccentricities. I hate to play favorites but, every so often, something about a particular fare enthralls me.

Brazil or Chill

"Could you come pick up Natalie at the restaurant?" a familiar voice spoke to me on the cellular. I'm still not sure who makes this regular call — the kitchen manager, I suppose.

"Sure," I replied. "I should be there in about 10. Little early tonight, isn't it?"

"Yeah, it's a slow week night, so we finished up early."

I've been driving Natalie from her dishwasher job to her apartment at South Meadow for the better part of the past year. She works a second job cleaning rooms at the Holiday Inn, but that's early in the day, before I go on duty. Anyway, I'm pretty sure she takes the bus to and from the day job. At working-class wages, you don't take unnecessary taxis.

Natalie is an immigrant from Brazil with a still-sketchy command of English, her first language being Portuguese. Lately her English has improved by leaps and bounds, so our small chats require less exaggerated pantomime than previously.

I pulled up to the restaurant and watched Natalie as she approached the taxi. She has a round, pleasing face, soft features and warm eyes. Everything about her is short — her legs, arms and fingers. Short, but strong: The muscles in her hands and forearms are noticeable.

"Hello, hello, hello," Natalie greeted me as she got in the front seat. As always, she was smiling like Christmas morning. I don't think I've met another person seemingly more delighted with life. The triple-hello I regard as her trademark sign-on. Given her limited English vocabulary, my guess is she compensates by repeating the words she does know two or three times.

"Hey there, Natalie," I replied. "How ya doing tonight? Working hard, huh?"

"Oh, yes, yes, yes," she said with a laugh. "Always working hard. Always."

I noticed for the first time that she sort of sung when she spoke. Conversing with her was like entering into that '60s French flick, *The Umbrellas of Cherbourg,* where all the dialogue is set to melody.

"It's tough to get ahead, isn't it? I remarked. "Working two jobs can't be easy for you."

"No, no!" she reacted with a vehemence that surprised me. "I don't mind working hard. This country is great! I have good apartment — nice and clean — and even after bills, I send money back to my family in Brazil."

Man, I thought to myself, anyone who starts taking life in America for granted should get out and talk to a recent immigrant. Even those of us hanging on at the lower rungs of the economic ladder have access to the basic necessities of life. Speak to some of our new Southeast Asian, African, East European or Tibetan neighbors if you think that's a small thing. I guess we can add Brazilian neighbors to that list as well.

I took the left onto Pine Street — the cabdriver's "friend." What other Burlington street runs for a couple of miles, with rarely a traffic jam and just two stoplights? The road was clear tonight with but a smidgen of slush and ice dotting the center line. I'm thankful for any winter day I don't have to negotiate snowy streets.

"Are you working straight through the whole winter," I asked, "or are you gonna take some time off?"

"No, no," she sang. "I have ticket to go São Paulo next week. I will get one month there. It too cold here, too cold!"

We turned into the South Meadow development and slowed to a crawl as we jounced through a series of speed dips. A small army of kids lives in these housing units, and the canyon-like dips were designed to keep them alive. Natalie, as far as I knew, lived alone and had no children.

"What will you do in Brazil?" I asked as we approached Natalie's apartment. "Did you say you have family down there?"

"Oh yes, oh yes!" she replied, her eyes sparkling at the thought. "I have many, many — how you say? — nephews and also the girls."

"Nieces, you mean?"

"Yes, yes, nieces. Many little *raparigas.*"

Natalie's eyes were misty as we pulled to a stop. What a soul-shaking decision it must be, I thought, to pick up and move to a new country. All the loved ones left behind. I don't know if I'd have it in me.

"The first thing when I get to São Paulo," Natalie spoke as she paid the fare, "do you know what is for me?" The smile on her face was irresistible.

"Tell me, Natalie."

"I go to the beach with my friends, and on that beach, in the night, we dance the samba."

Since this conversation with Natalie, every time I feel a blast of that cold air coming off the lake, I think of her on a sultry Brazilian shore, the water gently lapping onto the beach. It's dusk, the music is playing and she's laughing and dancing the samba. This picture is the secret layer that's been keeping me warm all winter.

Me 'n' Teddy

It was a drizzly, mid-November evening. As I watched the train conductor unload a series of overflowing, well-worn canvas bags, I thought to myself, *Could it be?*

A moment later I got my answer as a diminutive older man emerged from the train and our eyes met. Teddy is one of my favorite regular customers — if you can call a person I drive three or four times a year a "regular." His destination is Middlebury, which is a long haul, and we like each other. I think for these reasons I've qualified Teddy as a bona fide regular in the Hackie pantheon.

"Teddy, how you doin', brother?" I asked as I began to gather up his endless collection of belongings. He's a person with a terrific resistance to parting with any object that passes through his world — from this morning's Styrofoam coffee cup to last Tuesday's *USA Today*. Such a lifestyle, you can well imagine, necessitates a small army of duffle bags when you hit the road for a few weeks.

"Oh, just fine, yup, just fine. How are you?" Teddy's eyes are warm, moist and dark, and when he smiles at you the crinkles are off the chart. With his slightly hunched posture — I think he's in his seventies by now — and softly melodious yet gravelly speech, he brings to mind a composite of Yoda from *Star Wars* and Gollum from the *Lord of the Rings* trilogy. You might want to throw Danny DeVito into the mix, now that I think about it, because he's also got an East Coast, streetwise quality bubbling beneath the charm.

We squeezed all of the bags into the trunk, and Teddy settled into the front seat for the long ride south. "So tell me," I asked, "How's the team doing this year?"

"Well, they play in the spring, you know that?"

"Actually, I didn't. Lacrosse is a spring sport, huh? Makes sense I guess. So how'd they do this past spring?"

"Another wonderful year, yup. We went 17-2 for the regular season. Didn't win the tournament, unfortunately. That's after winning the national championship the previous three seasons, so it was a bit of a letdown. Great group of boys, though."

Teddy's been associated with Middlebury College sports for many years. Though I've asked, I'm still unsure of his status with the program. He might be a designated trainer or manager, something like that. Whatever his position, official or otherwise, I gather that he serves as an inspirational figure, especially to the lacrosse team. At the start of each new season, for example, the boys gathers around and Teddy gives a speech.

We puttered down Route 7 in a steady rain. Despite the poor driving conditions, I actually could have been going a little faster, but I was dogging it to maximize my Teddy time.

As we passed the Vergennes turn-off for Route 22A, Teddy turned to me with a wry smile and said, "You're a Red Sox fan, right?"

"That I am," I replied, "and may God have mercy on my soul. This year was another heart-breaker, that's for sure."

Teddy nodded his head sympathetically and said, "It reminded me of the Athletic-Cubs World Series of 1929. Boy, those poor Cubbies. In the fourth game they blew an eight-run lead in the seventh inning and, of course, went on to lose the Series. There's some serious heartache around that franchise, too."

"Ted, I know you're a big sports guy, but how the heck do you do you know these games going back to 1929? I gotta tell you, I'm impressed."

We eased down the winding road into Middlebury and took the usual stop at Cumby's, where Teddy loaded up on groceries. He's the only person I've seen do regular "supermarket shopping" at a convenience store. It's an expensive yet surprisingly relaxing way to food shop.

Teddy's apartment is on the second floor of a multi-family house. When we pulled in front, I began unloading his many bags and stacking them by the door while he fished around for the key. It was taking too long, and finally he said, "Sorry, but I just don't know what I've done with the key. There's a ladder around the back and I can get in through the window."

"Forget that Teddy, let me do it."

"All right," he said. "I'll hold the ladder."

In the misty rain, we walked around to the back of the house, stepping gingerly over the slick, matted leaves. Teddy held the ladder, which itself looked like it was constructed in 1929. No spring chicken myself, I carefully inched my way up the wobbly rungs, slid open the window and plopped into Teddy's bedroom.

Needless to say, there was stuff everywhere, boxes upon boxes. But amidst all the clutter, the place had a warm, cozy feeling. It felt like I had landed in the Shire, where the Hobbits live. I was kind of hoping Ted would invite me to stay for dinner. I could see us eating steamy platters of mutton and thick slabs of black bread. After the meal, we'd settle into comfy chairs before a fire and drink from big mugs of sweet tea while puffing on long-stemmed pipes. Oh, the stories we'd tell!

My fantasy was interrupted by Teddy knocking and calling for me. I unlocked the door and carried in all his bags. He then paid the fare with his usual generous tip, and said, "It was a pleasure being with you."

I looked into his twinkling eyes and replied, "The pleasure's all mine, Teddy. I mean it."

Getting Chubby

I drive by the old city armory many times a night. The ancient edifice on the corner of Main and Pine now houses office space and, until a recent fire, the dance club Sh-Na-Na's. Its massive brick exterior was constructed to withstand assault by enemy forces. For me, the notion of a time when protection was a matter of thicker walls is hard to imagine. But there it stands — a reminder of that long-lost world in brick and mortar.

Back in the day — and I'm talking way back in the last millennium — a venerable concert club occupied the Sh-Na-Na space. It was run by Chico Lager, who later went on to greater notoriety as the top executive at Ben & Jerry's. It was, by all accounts, one of the premier clubs for it's size in the country. Everyone from Sam & Dave to Suzanne Vega performed there. It was also a regular venue for some of the great local bands of the era: The Decentz, Pinhead, ZZebra and the mighty Killimanjaro.

It wasn't only musical acts that played this club. I saw Henny Youngman — the "King of the One-Liners" — perform there when he was already well past 80. Age hadn't even slightly impaired his comedic virtuosity; his timing was like Wayne Gretsky on a breakaway, Eric Clapton launching into a solo, Barishnykov leaping through the air. The audience, myself included, was literally rolling in the aisles, convulsed in laughter. And that is just one of my many happy memories of various evenings spent in this building.

The nightclub was called Hunt's, and I would often get calls to transport the visiting musicians around town. For a music lover like me, it was heaven.

"Jernigan, are you available?" It was just past midnight when the call came in from one of the club managers. The second set had probably just completed. "Some of the band members want to grab a bite to eat and I said you'd take them up to Howard Johnson's."

"You bet," I eagerly replied. "Is the man himself coming on this expedition? 'Cause this guy is one of my all-time favorites."

The manager chuckled. "What do *you* think, Jernigan?"

"All right! I'm on my way over."

Three men came out the front door of Hunt's and climbed into the back seat of the cab. Two of them appeared relatively young, but the third guy looked like he'd been at it from the beginning, and that would be the early '60s. This elder musician leaned forward and said, "Son, you better move the front seat back; he don't like to squeeze in, if you can dig it."

I dutifully obliged, and turned to fix my eyes upon the door of the club. When it swung open a moment later, the first thing I noticed were the pants: ruby-red, tight with a crease down the front that could slice provolone. Then the shoes: jet black and pointed like a dagger. And then the man: barrel-chested, mocha-brown skin and a smile that could guide wayward ships into safe harbor. It was Chubby Checker in the flesh.

Chubby eased into the shotgun seat and grinned at me. "How you been, cabbie?"

"I've been great, just great. It's an honor to drive you, sir — I mean that."

I experienced the goofy giddiness which accompanies, I suppose, the slightly surreal feeling of speaking face-to-face with the person you watched, at age 10, on your family's black-and-white television. The show would have been Dick Clark's "American Bandstand," and Chubby would have been Twisting "like he did last summer," and you would have been Twisting right along with him.

"Aw shucks," he replied. "That's all right, but don't give me any of that 'sir' stuff — Chubby's just fine."

"Thanks, Chubby." I said, beaming as we swung around and proceeded up the hill towards the all-night Howard Johnson's Restaurant. It was located were a Friendly's now operates, adjacent to the University Inn. "How was the show?" I continued. "What'd ya think of the crowd?"

Chubby twisted around in his seat. *No one could twist in his seat like Chubby Checker,* I thought to myself. He said, "What do you say, gentlemen? How do we like Burlington?"

"I'd say it was a good crowd," the senior musician replied from the rear seat. "We got 'em up shaking their booties, which is always pretty good for a bunch of white folks."

Laughter erupted in the taxi. Chubby said, "Yes sir, I agree with you, Tony. I like playing this town."

As we cruised up Main Street past the university, I couldn't help sneaking glances at my famous customer, a true pop-culture icon. The Twist was, and remains to this day, the biggest dance craze ever, and for my money it all comes down to Chubby Checker. Though he didn't invent it — and his first and biggest hit, "Let's Do The Twist," was a cover of an earlier recording by another artist — it was Chubby's immense charm and energy that sparked the Twist phenomenon. The guy's *joie de vivre* was galaxy-sized — I could feel it just sitting beside him.

When we pulled up to the entrance of the restaurant, Chubby turned and said, "Tony, if you'd be so kind, please pay the man." As Tony passed me the cash, Chubby stepped out of the vehicle. Before he headed into HoJo's, he bent down and flashed that smile at me through the open door, saying, "Cabbie, you be good now, all right?"

"I'll do my best, Chubby," I replied. "I will do my best."

I drove off with a big grin plastered across my face, the 10-year-old in me doing cartwheels.

My Sea Daddy

The call came from the bus terminal, which I hate. Half the time you arrive only to discover the fare is gone, having jumped in one of the many cabs which pass through the terminal all day long.

"Okay," I answered the caller's request, "I'll be there in 15 minutes, but promise me you'll wait for my cab, all right?"

"Oh yes! We promise. Just please come and get us; we need to catch a plane."

Twelve minutes later I arrived at the bus, and — surprise — no fare. I did notice an older man with thick, white slicked-back hair, smoking a cigarette on the terminal's outdoor deck area. Next to his feet sat a battered, gold-hinged foot locker. I called out, "Hey, how about you, buddy — you need a taxi somewhere?"

"I do, but I'm waiting for the one I called."

Thinking turn-about is fair play, I asked, "Well, where ya going?"

"I'm going to Port Henry. How much would *you* charge me?"

Port Henry is in New York across the Champlain Bridge — a terrific fare on a slow Wednesday afternoon. I know what the fleets are apt to charge for the run — about $80. It took me exactly three seconds to think this through and come up with my price.

"I'll take you for 60 bucks."

It took the man exactly two seconds to do his computation. It's what's known as a "no-brainer."

"You're on," he said with a grin. "The name's Rennie."

"Please to meetcha. I'm Jernigan."

The case fit — just barely — in the trunk, and Rennie got in the front with me. As we cruised south on Pine Street I further pinned down the destination.

"I know how to get to Port Henry all right, but once we get there do you know how to find your location?"

"Sure do, partner," he replied with a long-time-smokers' growl. "We're going to my nephew's house. I've visited there a few times. His mom — which would be my sister — died a couple months ago. I was out in the Gulf at the time. As soon as I got the news, I called and came up."

"You bussed all the way from the South?"

"Heck no," he replied. "I drove until my Crown Vic gave out in Tennessee. Engine exploded."

"No kidding? That's gotta be a bad thing."

"Yes indeedy," he said, with a raspy chuckle. "That *is* what you call a bad thing. Anyways, I caught a lift with a trucker up to Boston and took the Greyhound the rest of the way. I gave the trucker most of my gear; it was too much stuff to carry with me. Gave him a marvelous car jack. That was tough to part with."

This is my kind of guy, I thought to myself as we passed the traffic light in Shelburne Village. The heaviest Route 7 traffic began to dissipate after that. *Salt of the earth, and perhaps even an actual salt*, as I remembered what he had told me.

"So you said you were out in the Gulf. Are you working the oil rigs, or are you a sailing man?"

"No, I'm a sailor all right. More than 40 years now. Gonna retire pretty soon."

The movie *Forrest Gump* popped into my mind. "Are you a shrimper?" I asked.

"Nope. I mostly work on tugboats keeping watch on the oil rigs. The big rigs are required to have tugs keeping watch in case of fire." Rennie brought his fingertips softly together, and as I glanced over at him, a far-away look came over his eyes.

"Funny you ask, though," he continued, "'cause I did *start out* on a shrimp boat. I can remember it clear as day. Feller named Joe Slinker was the captain. Yeah, Ol' Joe was my sea daddy."

"Did you say, 'sea daddy?'"

"Sorry, partner — that's sea talk. We call the captain of your first boat your sea daddy. Some of those old boys can be brutal on newcomers, but Ol' Joe, he took me under his wing. We worked together quite a few times in those early years. Best boo-ray player I ever seen."

"That's some kinda card game they play down in Louisiana, right?"

Rennie let out a croupy guffaw. He sounded like a clangorous radiator on its last legs "That's not just 'some kinda card game,' brother. We talkin' boo-ray — the passion, pride and joy of the Bayou."

"Sorry, Rennie," I said chuckling along, "I'll try to remember that."

It was a beautiful ride through Addison County, this July weather being more than we could ask for. The windows were down and farm smells — wild flowers, newly-cut hay, Holsteins and field-spread manure — filled the air. After the long stretch east on Route 17, the towering Champlain Bridge came into sight, it's silver spans glistening in the late-afternoon sun. On days like this I almost feel guilty that I'm getting paid.

Port Henry's downtown bears the architecture of a mid-20th-century heyday, but signs of 21st-century retail activity are far and few between. Still, it doesn't feel depressed, like some other upstate New York towns. Plenty of people were on the street when we arrived, and the local creemee stand was going gangbusters. Rennie was pointing out various landmarks he recalled, as he directed me up a long hill running west out of the town center.

A few miles up, we turned into a steep driveway that ended at a modest brick house with an enormous aboveground pool attached to its rear deck. Even before we came to a stop, three little kids came bounding out of the water and ran squealing and dripping into Rennie's waiting arms. A man then came out the back door and leapfrogged the deck fence.

"Uncle Rennie!" the man said, giving him an affectionate squeeze around the neck with a husky forearm. "It's great to see you! We we're expecting you a couple days ago."

Well, *that's* a long story," Rennie replied with a laugh. "We'll get to it — and a few more, I suppose."

The two men managed to get the kids somewhat settled down, and Rennie pulled out his wallet to pay me.

"There's nothing like family, partner," he said handing me the fare. "Don't ever forget that."

I smiled, and replied, "Rennie, I sure won't."

A Valuable Commodity

For a few years in the mid-'80s, I regularly drove Dave Mamet. Yes, *the* Dave Mamet — playwright, screenwriter, director, essayist, acting teacher, novelist and renowned iconoclast. Dave owned a house outside of Plainfield with his then-wife, Lindsay Crouse — an actress of some repute herself — and a couple of times a month he would call me for transport to or from Burlington Airport.

I looked forward to these Mamet runs both for the obvious financial aspect — regular, lucrative long-distance fares are a boon to any cabbie — but just as much for the opportunity to simply hang out with Dave. In the beginning I was somewhat star-struck; although this was a few years before his string of successful Hollywood projects, he had already achieved national acclaim for his playwriting. Soon my awe faded — Dave didn't wear his celebrity like a badge — and I was left with the sheer enjoyment of spending time with one of our generation's great storytellers. I grew to think of him as the World's Most Interesting Acquaintance.

A typical Mamet piece of work is known for the world of men dramatically portrayed in all its brutal realism. You know — the misogyny, heartlessness, duplicity, etc. There's also, of course, the notorious choice of language. An actor friend told me this one: A panhandler approaches a man on a Chicago street. "Hey buddy, can you spare a buck?" The man replies, "'Neither a borrower nor a lender be' — William Shakespeare." The panhandler says, "'Fuck you' — David Mamet."

Perhaps based on the tone of his work, Dave himself has quite the public persona of the growling, contrarian tough guy. This didn't jive with my experience of him; I found him approachable, friendly, even warm. So much for media reputation.

Pick a subject, any subject, and Dave would have something original and compelling to say about it. Talking with him was the precise opposite of boring. I recall tasty conversations about darts technique, Goddard

College at the height of its late-'60s insanity, macrobiotics and hold'em poker. You name it.

"Are you working on anything now, Dave?" I asked him on one these memorable rides. (This question, I should point out, was rhetorical in that Dave was, and is, *always* working on something. Calling his output prodigious is an understatement.)

"Yeah," he replied, "as a matter of fact I'm writing a play."

"Could you tell me the gist of it?"

"Well, it's about a real estate office. The boss is running a contest for the agents." A sly grin appeared on his face. "Whoever sells the most properties in this new development over a certain period of time wins a new Cadillac. Whoever comes in second gets a set of steak knives. And whoever comes in third is fired."

Of course, what Dave had laid out for me, in primitive form, was the soon-to-be Pulitzer Prize-winning play — later made into a movie — *Glengarry Glen Ross.*

So that's kind of cool.

I also vividly recall our conversation upon his return from an L.A. trip he undertook in search of financial backing for his first directorial project.

"Jernigan, it's unbelievable out there," he said. "There's large office buildings filled with guys in suits. They live in mortal fear of OK'ing a project that ultimately goes south. Saying 'no' is the road to job security."

I could see he was just getting going, and I was all ears.

"And they're making all these inferences about not wanting to treat me — the great artiste, right? — as a commodity. Like they wouldn't want to 'insult' me. What they don't get is I have no problem being treated as a commodity; I just want to be treated as a valuable commodity."

Despite industry foot-dragging, the movie did get made. It's a great film, starring Joe Mategna, about one of Dave's principal obsessions: con men. They, i.e. the guys in the suits, forced him to change the title. I wish I could recall Dave's original title choice, but it was classy, something like the address of the bar where most of the action occurs, *1649 Broadway,* or some such. In any event, it's a fabulous movie: *House of Games.*

I think Dave still maintains his property up here. He's written stories and essays about Vermont, and his affection for the state, its people and natural beauty, is obvious and always eloquently expressed. In the fearless eye he casts on our culture, unswayed by fashion or conventional wisdom, it seems, to me anyway, that he has been decidedly influenced by the Vermont sensibility. Now, if he could only laugh at himself a bit more freely, see the whimsy in the conundrum, then we'd know the Vermont soul had fully taken hold.

For whatever reason, I don't hear from him any more. I remembering reading that he moved to Cambridge, Massachusetts, where he lives with his new wife. I miss driving him. Dave drove a cab in his hometown Chicago when he was a young man. As I now reflect upon it, perhaps that was the key to our connection. Never underestimate the "hackie bond."

Ferry Godmother

The caller said he needed a ride to the Essex ferry. "I'm your man," I replied. "By the 'Essex ferry,' you mean the ferry that leaves out of Charlotte, correct?"

The three Lake Champlain ferries are generally known by the New York towns they go to. It can be surprisingly confusing, so I've learned through the years to double-check with the fares to eliminate any ambiguity and missed connections.

"I'm sorry, but I'm from out of town, and I just arrived at the airport. I have no idea about 'Charlotte.' A family member is going to meet me at the Essex ferry dock, and she instructed me to take the 'Essex ferry.'"

"Good enough," I said. "There's an information booth right near the luggage belt. I'll meet you there in 15 minutes. What's your name?"

"George Cameron," he replied.

I was in the airport 10 minutes later. "Under-promise and over-deliver" — that's my business mantra. Scores of people were standing around awaiting their luggage, but no one was at the info booth save the man who staffs it, a diminutive woman and me. This lady was immaculately garbed in a tailored, dove-gray pants suit, with diamonds everywhere, and she had one of those dyed, blow-dried-and-sprayed, no-hair-out-of-place coiffures so favored by the country-club woman of means. It appeared that she too was waiting for something or someone, but, clearly, she was not George Cameron.

I had the booth guy page my fare, but it was looking increasingly like a no-show. Maybe George decided to rent a car, I speculated. I was about to cut my losses and vamoose when the lady turned and spoke to me.

"You're a cabdriver, right? Could you possibly take me to the Plattsburgh ferry? My driver hasn't shown up."

"You bet," I said, counting my luck. "This is perfect, because my fare didn't show up. It's kismet."

"Well, I call it something else," she said, as I tipped her two bulging bags onto their wheels, and together we headed outside to my taxi. The lady got in the front with me. She sat there beaming, and appeared hyper-alert.

"I told you it was something more than kismet that brought us together, didn't I?"

"You sure did," I said. I had a sneaking suspicion where this was headed.

"Well, I made a life-long friend three years ago, and he never fails to look out for my welfare. It was Jesus that got me this ride."

Bingo, I thought. *Here we go.*

"I spent years trying one thing or another, every type of self-help seminar, yoga — you name it. Nothing brought me peace. But then I received Jesus Christ into my heart and all my questions were answered."

"Who are you visiting in New York?" I asked in a blatant attempt to change the subject before she really hit high gear. I have complete respect for anyone's spiritual path. Anything in this hard, cruel world that brings you peace and equilibrium, I say, "Glory be, and go for it." I just have a hard time with any manner of proselytizing. In matters of the spirit, it seems to me, you shouldn't have to induce anyone, like you're selling a Buick or something.

"My son Jason is competing in an Iron Man race in Lake Placid. I don't know what happened to the driver he arranged to meet me. Praise the Lord, Jesus took care of that problem."

"You have some kind of southern accent, I'm guessing. Is this your first time up here to Yankee country?"

"Heavens, no," she said. "I'm a Dallas girl, but my husband and I moved to his family's property in Rockland, Maine, three years ago. We're recently separated now, and I'm back in Texas. He was always angry and depressed, and kept trying to bring me down to his level. I just could not live that way, and I prayed and prayed, until Jesus told me to leave him."

"Really?" I said.

"Yes, sir. I have a boyfriend now, from Israel of all places. He's 36, much younger than me — I have a daughter who's 31 — but we're a match made in heaven. He's married also, but not for long. In Dallas, he's a successful builder and contractor, and I tell him: 'Now the two loves of my life are both Jewish carpenters!'"

We chatted amiably for the next while, touching upon the sublime and the profane. Mostly, she spoke and I listened. Soon we had passed the Sand Bar State Park, and were motoring down the long causeway leading over to

South Hero. Boats were out everywhere on this balmy summer day, bobbing on the gentle waves.

I was beginning to take a shine to this woman. She was so out there, weird and inconsistent in her beliefs and actions. Just keeping up with her story was challenging. Being with her was refreshing in some odd way I couldn't quite put my finger on.

We arrived at the ferry dock just as they had let on the last car and were about to push off. I stepped on it, pulling right up to the big boat. I yelled up at the two ferry people as they were dragging the big chain across the stern, "Room for one more walk-on?"

One of the two — a ferrywoman — looked towards her shipmate, nodded at him, then said to me, "Sure, there's always room for a walk-on."

On my own, it would have taken a few minutes to lug the two heavy bags onto the boat, but with the help of the two deckhands, we had them aboard in a jiffy. The Texan, bubbly as ever, paid the fare, threw in a good tip and scurried up the ramp. In the next moment, the engines stirred to life, and the ferryboat began to move.

I looked up, and the lady was energetically waving goodbye to me. She called out, "Jesus loves you!"

I smiled back from the window of my taxi, placed my palms together in front of my face, and bowed my head. I'm not sure where that came from, but in the moment it just felt right.

Right-Hand Man

For the longest time, I had no idea who he was or what he did. All I knew was, he would arrive on the afternoon Montpelier bus about once a month, and transfer to my taxi for the trip to the airport. He was a big man, of or nearing retirement age, but there was no hesitancy in his gait — he moved with purpose.

He would acknowledge me when we connected at the bus terminal, with a nod that let me know that he remembered me. Though he never made small talk during our rides, he didn't strike me as snobbish, or even standoffish. He would simply ride in the back seat, a reflective look in his light blue eyes. Sometimes he would carefully remove a document from his well-used, leather briefcase, and read it over, slightly squinting. He seemed an intensely private man.

Once — just once — I summoned the courage, and asked him where he flies. "Atlanta, Georgia," he responded, in a sonorous bass tone.

After the better part of a year and quite a few of these trips, my curiosity began to seriously mount. What it was about this man, this particular fare, that so stimulated my interest, I'm hard put to say. There was something about him, and again, I find myself going back to the way he carried himself. I've heard a word used in the description of an individual of societal moment and intellectual depth and, despite having never really spoken with him, I would have applied it to this man: *gravitas*. He radiated it.

But even as my curiosity built, I kept quiet, honoring his privacy. Though I'm normally chit-chatty, I can recognize and respect a person who is not. Plus, we all know what killed the cat.

Finally, on one of our rides together, I saw him straighten up in his seat. "So, how do you like cab driving?" he asked.

"Well," I replied slowly, trying to squelch any sign of over-eagerness. "I like it just fine. I'm my own boss, I enjoy driving, and I get to meet a lot of interesting folks."

"That's a big plus in life, to like what you do," he said, relaxing back into his seat.

Sensing his expansive mood, I wasn't going to let this relative explosion of volubility pass untapped. The opportunity may not come again, I thought. *Carpe diem*, and all that.

"So," I ventured with near giddy expectation, my months of speculation on the verge of resolution, "what kinda work do you do?"

"I work for the Carter Center," he replied without hesitation. "It's a foundation established by Jimmy Carter."

"OK," I said. "OK, I've heard of that. You're active on issues of world peace and reconciliation. Is that right?"

I watched a smile come over his face in the rear-view mirror. "Yes, that probably encapsulates our mission in a phrase or two."

This was intensely intriguing to me. I've always had profound admiration for Jimmy Carter. I guess it's conventional wisdom that he wasn't terribly effective as a president, but his life's work, including both before and especially post-presidency, is a model of integrity and humility. For my money, these two qualities are in short supply in modern public life. Jimmy Carter is one of those guys who inspires me to try to do some good in my miniscule corner of the world.

"So whatcha working on currently? Where's the President focusing his attention?" It felt right to refer to Jimmy Carter by the honorific title attached for life to anyone achieving our highest elected office.

"Well, a lot of focus is still on the establishment of a World Court. This would function under the auspices of the U.N. and would deal with, among other things, the trial of war criminals accused of crimes against humanity. Unfortunately, the United States has been the chief roadblock in this effort."

The Ho-Hum Motel signaled the left turn to the airport. Although I've passed this motel a half-dozen times a day for 25 years, I still find the name amusing.

There was, however, one unresolved matter. My curiosity was not yet fully sated, and time was a-wasting. "So, I haven't asked you," I said, "what exactly do you do at the Carter Center?"

He didn't answer immediately, and I could see him stroking his chin with his left hand. Then he said, "I work closely with the President on a variety of organizational and policy issues."

As we pulled into the airport horseshoe, it hit me: This is Carter's right-hand man. I just knew it. His answer was somewhat vague, but that was just the humility talking.

"Nice chatting with you," he said with a warm smile, as he paid the fare.

"Likewise," I replied. "See ya next time."

I watched him step out of the cab, and stride through the sliding door of the terminal. I had felt an inexplicable attraction to this man for months, and now it had grown into genuine admiration. If, in my imagination, I would construct a person whom Jimmy Carter might choose as a close confidante and advisor, that person would look exactly like the man I had just dropped off.

Pulling out of the airport, I felt oddly elevated, as if, in some sense, I had just experienced the thoughtful and compassionate presence of former president Jimmy Carter himself.

Ballplayers

These young men are big. Not huge, like football players, nor tremendously tall, like the basketball players from the local college teams. But they are tall, well-built, muscular guys, fresh-faced with a jaunty bounce to their step, an eagerness to their gaze. They revel in the nightly party that is downtown Burlington, but like Cinderella at the ball, they dare not stay till the end. If they fail to make it back to their hotel by midnight curfew, the manager will have their hide. They are 19 or 20 years old, and they get paid to play baseball. At their level of the profession — Single-A — you keep your nose clean and play your heart out every game.

Single-A leagues are the lowest rung on the Major League "farm system," so named because the business of the farm system is "growing" ballplayers. Sticking with the metaphor, the farm teams at the Single-A level are engaged in a weeding-out process: A prospect either moves up to Double or Triple-A within a year or two, or he is released. The quickness, the power, the uncanny ability required to compete and survive is, to me, nearly unfathomable and, in fact, less than 5% of minor leaguers ever ascend to "The Show," player slang for the Major Leagues.

These Single-A guys have already proven themselves in Little League and American Legion ball; they are the stars of their high school and college teams, the cream of their regions, cities and states. It's as if Harvard University's entering freshmen, the elite of the nation's high school graduates, knew that expulsion awaits the vast majority of their classmates, those not achieving the very highest grades. The system is Darwinism at its most brutal.

But these young men, in town to play our Vermont Expos — they're cocky. From that day as little boys when they first picked up a bat or threw a ball, they've imagined themselves as Major Leaguers. So far everything's proceeded according to plan; the long odds mean nothing to them. That is, at least until the manager calls them into the office at the end of the season.

"You folk here think this is party? Y'all come on down to N'warlens, Mardi Gras time. That there is party."

The speaker is sitting with his buddy in the rear seat. The two of them are ballplayers. (Somehow, I just know.) Because he's forced to leave downtown early, his sentiments reveal the tinge of sour grapes. Not to take a thing away from the Bacchanalia of Mardi Gras; it's just that — put it this way — our own Queen City ain't chopped liver when it comes to merrymaking. He has these pale blue eyes, I mean nearly translucent like the eyes of a Siberian Husky, and a buzz-cut of blonde hair, Marine-style. The thought breezes in that 35 years ago this kid's in the jungles of Southeast Asia — no deferment back then for a great fastball. I bet more than a few potential big leaguers never came back from that war. For some reason, this stray thought hits me with a shot of ineffable sadness.

"Hey cabbie," he continues, mercifully breaking off my bleak reverie. "You tell me, man. Where you think me and my boy here come from?" His friend was, like him, big, brawny and blonde.

"Well," I reply, "if you're not from Louisiana, you're pulling off one heck of a good impersonation. Your teammate, I'm guessing — down south also?"

"Good guess, brother. He from Atlanta Gee Ay. That us all right — a couple of big, dumb, good ol' boys."

I get a kick out of that, the easy, self-deprecatory humor of southern guys. Feeling expansive, I broach my single favorite subject in this whole wide world: Baseball. "So what do you guys play?"

"Well, we're both pitchers," he replies. "I start, and ol' Derrick here, he the reliever."

"So what's your money pitch?" I ask.

"My money pitch, huh?" he says with a chortle. "I got a big, bad-ass curveball. The manager, he call it 'Public Enemy Number One.' If I'm in a jam, men on base, he come on out to the mound, and he tell me, 'Quit fooling around now, Billy, and just throw that Public Enemy Number One.' That just about kills me every time he say that. But it works, dang it; it pump me up something fierce."

"What about you, Derrick," I ask, speaking for the first time to the other young man, who hasn't said a word to this point. "What's your best pitch?"

In the rear-view mirror I see a bemused grin come across Derrick's face. He takes a good few seconds before responding. Fast talking is not a southern trait. "I'll tell you what," he says with a slow, silken drawl. "I jus' throw strikes. The pitching coach tells me, 'You want to make it to the Bigs, you jus' keep throwing strikes.' So that's my plan — throwing strikes."

At the hotel, Billy and Derrick split the fare and throw in a good tip. These ballplayers, despite being young kids from all over the country, often small towns, they still know to take care of the cabdriver. I got to believe the coaches fill them in on this sort of thing — the dos and don'ts of life on the road.

These young men are ballplayers. Many sports are played with a ball, but when someone says, "ballplayer," the game is understood. It's baseball, and the young men have been at it for a 150 years. "Go ahead, Billy. Throw 'em your best pitch — Public Enemy Number One."

6

BATTLE OF THE SEXES

The relationship bonding of a man and woman in a positive way for longer than 72 hours is, to me, one of life's genuine miracles.

In my taxi, night after night, the boys and the girls play out this eternal dance in all its glorious, gory aspects.

Foreplay

"What was that all about?" he says. "Why does she have to be like that? So what if it was the coat room; we were just *talking*, for God's sake."

The two of them, a man and woman in their early thirties, are decked out in semi-formal evening clothes. They sit in the back of my taxi as we head down Route 7 towards Shelburne. At two in the morning, Shelburne Road is a thing of beauty, what with the lights all a'blinking and only the stray car or truck for traffic. The radio's on, but I'm eavesdropping on the conversation. This is a good one, because something's going on here, something between the lines.

"Well you know how she is, John." the woman chimes in. "I could totally see her point of view. It's like her sister's big night and all, and like you *are* her husband. She expects your attention on an occasion like this. I mean, maybe you *could* call it a *little* over-dependent, but I totally understand where she's coming from."

At this point in the proceedings, I've unobtrusively adjusted the rear-view mirror. Maybe I'm kidding myself, but I really don't consider myself overly nosey. This is my excuse: It's late, I'm bored and this conversation is shaping up as a beaut.

John sits back in his seat, a pensive look upon his face. He then turns, thoughtfully, to address his traveling companion. "Oh, man, Jill. As always, you're *so* right. I don't know what the hell's wrong with me. It's just that she knows how far back me and you go, and you figure she could cut me a little slack."

Jill smiles knowingly. "You are just too sweet," she says. "You really do try to be understanding. Sometimes I wonder if she realizes just how lucky she is to have a man like you."

"Just storming out like that," he continues. "I just don't think that's called for. I guess she was planning to stay over at her sister's tonight, anyway, but still, it makes me look like a total pinhead."

He's still voicing the upset feeling, but John's eyes have brightened. It looks like he really took in Jill's last remark; the "man like you" part is circulating through his ego system and it's feeling pretty good.

Jill's hand now moves to John's knee. Let's not read anything into it, though. They go back so far, and all.

"Anyone who thinks you're a 'pinhead' doesn't know the real John," she says. "Just let it go."

With that, John bows his head and gets a boyish, crooked grin, all bashful and charming. Jill is wearing a satiny, red strapless to stunning effect. She gives him an exaggerated shrug of the shoulders and a big, warm smile. I'm not sure, but I think it's their private semaphore for, *I'm OK; you're OK; all is well.*

"Hey, that band was great, weren't they?" John says, moving out of *mea culpa* into more lighthearted terrain. "You do a mean *Electric Slide,* you know that?"

"We always danced great together," she replies softly. "That was true back at UVM, and it's true today." The hand has returned to the knee, or it could be the thigh. I can't say for sure as the angle of the mirror fails me below the waist.

Friendship is a wonderful thing, isn't it? It's so special when friends are such great dance partners. And here's where the dance steps get very subtle, very complex.

We're approaching John's home in Shelburne, and he says, "I don't know what it is, but I'm not the least bit tired. How about you? Do you want to come in for a nightcap?"

"John, I was hoping you'd ask!" she says. "Me too, I'm feeling so much — I don't know — energy tonight."

Energy is a good thing. I wish I had more of it, although one wonders why these two good friends need all this energy at two in the morning at John's place with his wife sleeping over the sister's.

The layers of the mind are astounding. The capacity for one part of ourselves to deceive another part of ourselves is a bit of mental gymnastics I've observed in my own life. The greater heartache, I've come to realize, has not stemmed from lying to others, but lying to myself.

I used to be a betting man and, out of habit, I still mentally run the numbers. If pressed, I would give these odds of Jack and Jill "going up the hill" tonight: 9 out of 10 says they do it. But as they exit the taxi and walk towards the door, I have no doubt they are both telling themselves, earnestly, that they're only having a drink and some small talk. And, maybe they will do just that. Really, what do I know? It's truly none of my business, but we cabbies see and hear it all.

Boy Crazy

"You're a man. Tell me . . . What does it say when you take a girl to a wedding? That, like, means something, right?"

The question was posed by the woman in her early twenties sitting next to me. This was not the first time I'd had Thelma in my cab, and the conversational subject is always the same: her chaotic and ultimately tragic love life. I'm loathe to get into it, not because I'm without sympathy, but having visited this domain with her too many times, I know that she's — well, stuck would be the best way to describe it.

"Thelma, I really couldn't tell ya," I replied, carefully choosing my words. "I really don't know if there's any rules about things like that."

Looking over at her, I could see that my evasive response was not going over too well. For some reason, this young woman fully expected her cabdriver to sort out her relationship quandaries — in itself not exactly sign of emotional stability.

"Look," I continued, "I'm a thousand years old. You see what I'm saying? I mean, really — what the hell do I know about this stuff?"

We were *en route* to Kennedy Drive to visit one boyfriend — the recalcitrant wedding escort, I gathered — when her phone rang, playing the riff from "American Woman": Da-Da-Da-Da-Da, Da-Dum. *Just Perfect,* I thought.

"No, Joey, I'm, like, just hanging around downtown," she lied to the caller. "Where are you? . . . *Yes,* I want to see you. *C'mon,* you know that. Buell Street? OK, I'll be right there."

Here we go again, I thought to myself. I turned, looked at my customer and awaited the inevitable. Sure enough, a sheepish grin came upon her face, and she said, "Um, I've changed my mind. Take me to Buell Street, please."

This turn of events was anything but a surprise. It seems like every time I drive Thelma, she works the phones and we zigzag all over town.

"Thelma, did he tell you what number? 'Cause Buell goes for a few blocks."

"Shit, I'll call him back and get it."

She punched the numbers; it rang and rang until the voice mail picked up. "Joey, call me back, OK? It's me. I need the apartment number on Buell."

Then, out of nowhere, she turned to me and blurted out, "I'm a pretty girl, right? Don't ya think so?"

I pulled into a bank parking lot on Dorset Street and swung the vehicle around to head back towards Buell. This, on the chance that Paramour #2 would indeed get back to her with the address, a dubious assumption given her track record. I glanced over at Thelma who was looking at me wistfully, her eyes shining with vulnerability and hope.

Thelma's cultural heritage is Indian, or maybe Thai — it's hard for me to tell. She's short and utterly curvaceous, and this night she was wearing a black skirt that did full justice to the word "mini." Her top was a skimpy, scarlet camisole and, like the skirt, this article of clothing was doing everything it was designed to do.

I'm a typical man, I suppose, and not immune to the allure of such a presentation. But, like Jerry Lewis on his Labor Day Telethon, a woman can oversell the appeal. Thelma was trying way too hard. When the bid for male attention goes to these extremes, it's probably a safe bet that it's not really about sexual desire. You don't have to be Freud to detect the deeper need screaming beneath the surface. One unflinching look into Thelma's eyes revealed that in spades.

Still, I had to respond to her plaintive question; it was floating in the cab like a pregnant cloud. We came to a stoplight on Williston Road. "Thelma," I said softly, consciously trying to diffuse the feeling of drama and urgency this person carried around with her like a purse. "For one thing, you're not a girl. You're a woman. All right? And the sooner you stop worrying about all these guys and start taking care of your own self, the better off you'll be."

"Thank you *sooo* much," she gushed. "Like, how true is what you just said? I swear, my brother tells me the *same* thing! So, thank you, and I'm gonna —"

"Da-Da-Da-Da-Da, Da-Dum." It was another call for the "American Woman."

"Hang on a sec," she said, her moment of self-reflection, as it were, over as quickly as it arose. "This could be Joey!"

She snapped open her cell phone, brought it up to her ear and said, "Oh, c'mon, you can't get the number? Like, how hammered are you? . . . OK, pick me up there; that'd be fine."

Thelma stashed the phone back in her purse and said, "Drop me off at Spillane's Mobil. Joey's gonna come get me there. This is awesome — I've been trying to hook up with this guy all summer!"

"What about the guy on Kennedy Drive?" I asked. Why I even cared, I have no idea. I guess I was smack into Thelma's machinations, yet again. I'm a sucker for the drama, and realistically that's not going to change anytime soon.

"Oh, yeah. I suppose I should call him back. He did take me to his cousin's wedding, after all."

"Yup, that would be nice," I sighed, and turned into Spillane's.

Decoupling

"Aw, Jeez," my customer said, rifling through his jacket pockets. "Is there a place we can stop to get cigarettes along the way?"

"At this point, not really, man," I replied. We were *en route* to the man's Woolen Mill apartment in Winooski, and had just reached the point where Pearl Street turns into Colchester Avenue. "I mean, nothing along the way. And, to be perfectly honest about it, I'm trying to keep moving this time a night. You know, last call and all that."

"No problem whatsoever. Just get me home, then."

"Thanks for the understanding," I said, glancing over at the middle-aged guy sitting next to me. He was very smartly dressed — causally, but everything looked new or close to it, and very top-of-the-line. It was uncommon for a person his age to remain downtown for the duration; the post-midnight crowd is generally limited to the those south of 30. The exceptions to this rule, I've found, are the certified alcoholics and the newly-divorced.

"I just signed the papers today giving the house to my wife and kids," the man said, as if he had just read my mind. "The whole thing still seems so unreal." His tone reflected the way men of my generation tend to express strong, unwelcome emotions: a jumble of bitterness, anger, irony and, beneath it all, a sorrow that could fill Lake Champlain.

"That's too bad, man," I said. "Must be a huge adjustment."

"I don't know what the hell I'm doing, to tell you the truth. All these years I worked my ass off, just for her and the kids. And now this. Those poor kids. My poor wife, really. The whole thing is a friggin' mess."

"What kinda work do you do?" I jumped in, quickly steering the conversation away from the raw emotions — a zone I'm not exactly comfortable hanging out in.

"Well, I'm sure you know my business," he replied, naming one of the well-established local contractors in the building trades. "It's all been going down the toilet lately. I've been so preoccupied with the divorce, I haven't been able to give the business the attention it requires. We're down to just 16 full-time employees."

"It'll come back up," I said, trying to console him in some small way. "The building trades tends to be cyclical anyway."

As we crossed the Winooski Bridge, he said, "Hey, I hate to ask, but would you mind shooting up the hill to Chuck's Mobil? I really need to pick up some Lucky Strikes."

"Lucky Strikes, huh? You ain't fooling around. I used to smoke Camels, myself. I mean, before there were a dozen filtered varieties and they started marketing them to teenagers."

I bore right through the roundabout, dropping all my urgency about the delay. *The poor guy's getting divorced and he needs his cigs*, I figured. As we passed the huge construction site for the Winooski redevelopment project, he said, "I was asked to bid on a big chunk of this thing, but I couldn't get bonded." He shook his head and exhaled audibly. "That's how bad things have gotten."

We pulled into Chuck's, and I watched him enter the store and make the buy. Stepping outside, he paused for a moment and tapped the edge of the Luckys on his palm, compacting those non-filters before tearing open the top of the pack.

We glided down the long hill back towards the Woolen Mill. Just as we passed over the train tracks, he asked, "Do you believe in God?" This was a slightly jarring question, seemingly coming out of nowhere. Then it occurred to me that divorce evokes just this kind of soul-searching.

"Yes, I do," I replied.

"I guess I do, too," he said, "But as hard as I try — and don't think I haven't — I just can't figure out what God is doing with my life. Like, what could possibly be the plan?"

"Boy, that's a tough one." I said. "Maybe stuff just happens sometimes. You gotta keep the faith though, doncha think?"

"Yup, you have to keep the faith. Thanks for listening to me gripe, by the way. Where are you from, anyway?"

"Well, I grew up in New York City, but I consider this my true home."

"Hey, you *are* a Vermonter, then. And that's from somebody whose family goes back about five generations up here."

"Thank you, man," I replied, feeling like I was about to get misty-eyed myself. "I take that as just about the highest compliment."

We eased to a stop in front of the Woolen Mill apartments, a known way station for divorcing men who have the bucks. He paid the fare and said, "You sure I can't offer you a cigarette?"

"Thanks, but I don't smoke."

"Hey, I don't either," he said, laughing. "I've just taken it up since the divorce."

"Really?" I said, laughing along with him. "Well, I say, 'What the hey!'"

The Pick-Up

The Independence Day celebration drew hordes of people to downtown Burlington — the appeal of fireworks never grow old. I took a couple of hours off from driving to partake in the festivities with my fellow citizens. It was fun to hear the sounds, to see the lights, to "ooh-and-aah" with the crowd.

After the post-fireworks traffic gridlock had abated, I moseyed back to my cab, flicked on the taxi light and returned to the fray. The remainder of the night went smoothly: streams of business and little rancor. Everyone I drove seemed in jolly spirits, and why not? We're all Americans and it was our birthday.

As the night wound down, I was hailed by two trim women, one with shoulder-length, streaked blonde locks, the other a brunette with a pixie haircut. The blonde woman wore one of those tubular neon necklaces that have become synonymous, for some reason, with 4th of July celebrations.

They were giggling as they splashed into the rear seat and asked to go to the new condo apartments near the Lime Kiln Bridge in South Burlington.

"You know what?" I said as we ascended the Main Street hill. "During the Great Flood of 1927, every single bridge on the Winooski River was washed away except for the Lime Kiln Bridge. That's 'cause it's so high above the water."

The blonde woman managed to stop giggling for a second, looked up and said, "Fascinating," before immediately going back to talking with her friend. *I'm a fount, all right,* I thought to myself. *"Fascinating Customers Since1980"* should be the tagline on the side of my door. The woman then said, "OK, Jennifer, let's go ahead and do it. But, like, how scandalous are we?"

"Ya only live once," Jennifer replied, scooting forward in her seat. "Mr. Cabbie," she said, "could you swing back to Church Street? I guess about the corner of Maple would be a good place to start. We're trying to find two cute guys we were just talking to."

"You sure about this?" I asked skeptically. This had "wild goose chase" written all over it.

"Oh, we're sure," Jennifer replied. "C'mon — go, go, go. They were walking down lower Church when we left them."

I took the right at Willard, and then another quick right onto Maple. We came down the hill up to the intersection with Church and, sure enough, two men were in the crosswalk.

"Omigod!" the blonde yelped, barely able to contain herself. "That's them, that's them!"

I pulled to the curb, lightly tapped the horn and beckoned to them from my window. They were handsome men, I had to admit, both tall with dark hair and chiseled features. They looked Latin, or maybe Arab — something interesting, in any event. One of them made a brushing-away motion with his hand, thinking I was trying to solicit a taxi fare.

"No, man," I called out. "C'mere. I got two women in this cab who are interested in you guys."

They looked at each other for a moment, as the import of what I had just imparted sunk in. Here's where one difference between men and women revealed itself: They couldn't get into the cab fast enough. For men — if I may speak for my less evolved sex — this is a no-brainer. One hopped in the back with the girls, the other took the shotgun seat.

"Hey, we know you!" the guy in the back said as he settled in. He did in fact have a Middle Eastern accent of some sort. "We were just talking to you in front of Manhattan Pizza."

"Well, boys," Jennifer began, adopting the tone of a schoolmarm, a hilarious choice given the decidedly indecorous circumstances. "We've decided to continue the evening, if you would so kind as to accompany us back to our apartment."

For a moment there was a stunned silence in the vehicle. The guys had just hit the lottery; these were two attractive and vivacious women. The smile on my seatmate's face was ear to ear. "Ladies," he said, 'we would like nothing better."

"What's a matter with your friend in the back here?" the blonde woman asked. "He seems a little freaked out."

I glanced at the rear-view mirror and, indeed, the guy back there did appear anxious.

"Ahmed," he spoke up to his friend in the front seat. "You know — we have our plans. We must get going tomorrow morning by six."

Jennifer made a couple of tsking sounds. "That's too, too bad, boys. I really think we could have had some fun."

We were still sitting, at this point, on the corner of Maple and Church. My seatmate looked stricken. "*Pssst*, Ahmed," I whispered to him. "Tell this to your clueless wingman in the back: 'Our plans have changed.'"

The smile returned to Ahmed's face. "Mousad," he said, pivoting in his seat. "Guess what, my friend? Our plans have changed."

Mousad leaned forward in this seat and said, "But Ahmed, what about — "

"My *friend*," Ahmed cut him off, lifting one finger, "there are no 'buts.' Listen to me carefully: Our plans have changed."

With that, Mousad finally came to his senses, and relaxed back into his seat next to his brand new friends. "OK," he said with a laugh. "I suppose you have made your point."

"All right!" Jennifer said. "Mr. Cabbie, back to the Lime Kiln Bridge. And you guys should really know this — it's the only bridge untouched by the Great Flood of 1927."

Jennifer winked at me in the mirror, and I chuckled. *It's so rewarding*, I thought, *when I can provide a little historical perspective.*

Nose Job

As I took the corner onto lower Church Street, I saw four police officers on the sidewalk by the courthouse surrounding a young man. I'm not above rubbernecking when I spot a good street drama, so I pulled into the convenient taxi stand at the side of Manhattan Pizza, cut the ignition and cracked my window.

One of the cops was up in the face of the guy, who was yelling and gesturing forcefully. About 10 feet away, a blonde-haired young woman stood watching with tears in her eyes, hands on her cheeks. All of the officers, even the one receiving the brunt of the guy's wrath, seemed quite relaxed, even placid.

Though they're omnipresent on the streets during the late-night bar hours, the Burlington Police take a mellow approach to law enforcement. They're constantly interacting with the young people around them and, when breaking up the bar fights, I've observed how they work to diffuse the conflict rather than coming in guns blazing, so to speak. I've seen it many times.

"Hey, buddy," the cop said evenly, staring directly into the eyes of the distraught young man. "Look around. You're the only one shouting here."

"But I told ya what happened!" the guy snapped back. "I told ya he — "

"I don't wanna hear it," the cop interrupted. "You got a choice right now, but the window of opportunity is closing fast. Why don't you grab a cab — call it a night — and we won't take any further action. Hey, there's one at the stand."

The two of them looked in my direction. *Great,* I thought, *now* I've *entered the drama.* I nodded my head, and the guy called to the blonde-haired woman, "Tina — are you comin' with me or what?"

Tina slowly raised her head from her hands. "Sure, Brian," she replied softly, barely audible over the street hubbub. "Are you sure that's what you want?"

"Do whatever you want," he replied. "I'm getting the hell out of here."

Brian crossed the street, Tina following behind. The two of them got into the back of my cab. For a moment neither said a word. Brian was holding his right hand over his nose, and now, at closer range, I noticed blood oozing slightly from a cut under his eye.

"I've had it with you!" he yelled. "What the hell was that about, Tina? Just what was I supposed to do?"

"Hey, folks" I leaped in. If this was going to be a lover's quarrel, I wanted the ride underway and over as soon as possible. "Couldja give me an address, OK?"

"Williams Road in Mallet's Bay, I guess," Tina replied.

"Yeah, that's fine, Tina. You go home. Cabbie, take me up to the emergency room. My nose is broken."

"Brian," she said. "What do you mean? Your nose can't be broken." Her voice carried an anguished mix of wishing and pleading. It didn't sound like she truly had any idea whether or not her boyfriend's nose was busted. "You're fine, Brian. I know you're fine."

"Is that right, Tina? Well feel this, all right — feel this."

He dropped his hand from his face, pointed to and gingerly rubbed a small bone where the nose meets the cheek. It was protruding unnaturally; if forced to guess, I'd have said he was right about the break. It looked pretty bad.

"Well then I'm going with you."

"*Wonderful*, Tina. Whatever you say."

"E.R. it is," I said, swinging the vehicle out into the road.

"Why were you kissing that guy? What's his name — Jake? How the hell do you think it makes me feel? I gotta face those guys every day. I look like a freakin' moron now!"

In the rear-view I saw Tina edge closer to Brian, lifting her arms as if to embrace him.

"Get the hell away from me!" Brian barked, shoving aside her arms. "You're a slut; I don't want anything to do with you anymore."

"Brian, I told you. It was nothing." Tears were running down Tina's cheeks. "What else can I say? It was nothing."

For a couple of blocks, there was no sound from the back except Tina's muffled crying. In my mind, I was trying to decide who was right, like some hackie Judge Judy. Don't ask me why — you play out a scene like this in a cab, you're going to get the cabbie involved, if only mentally. It was distressing to witness but, if you think about it, it's been going on since Anthony and Cleopatra.

"Give me something to work with, Tina," Brian started it up again as we passed the university. "That's all I'm asking; give me something to work with."

"Jake's an old boyfriend," Tina replied. "That's all. I was just being friendly."

"Oh, that's great. What's that supposed to make me feel better? I've had it with you. It's over Tina. You're history."

We took the right into the Fletcher Allen complex. The place is undergoing massive expansion and renovation, and the traffic flow is in constant flux. Every time I take somebody there, I have to follow the directional signs to see where the emergency room entrance is that week.

I pulled as close as I could to the door. "That'll be seven-fifty if you're both getting off here."

"You go ahead to Colchester." Brian said, barely glancing at Tina. "It's just me getting out."

"I don't even have any money on me," Tina said between what were now sobs.

"Jeez," Brian said, shaking his head. I thought I detected a small break in his wall of anger and admonishment. "I guess you're coming with me then."

Brian paid the fare and, without speaking, the two of them got out and walked side by side, toward the E.R. door.

Driving back downtown, I wondered what Brian was going to say when the attending physician began examining his nose and asked, "OK, why don't you tell me what happened?"

There are a shorter and longer versions of this old story, but they all begin something like this: "Well, doc, I was at the club, and I saw this guy kissing my girl . . ."

Party Down

"There's three of us tonight. We're going to a party on — Jen, what's the street that we're headed to? You have the address, right? Sorry, about this, Jernigan. We're real organized here."

I recognized the caller as Zooey, one of the many UVM students I count as regular customers.

"No problem," I said. "You're the girls from Harris-Millis, right? Going to a party in the middle of exam week? All's I can say is, 'Tsk, tsk.'"

"Wait a gosh, darn second there, dude. Give us a break! We've been studying non-stop for days; tonight we're just blowing off a little steam, that's all."

"Well, in that case," I replied with a chuckle, "I'll be there in 10."

"Thanks, and Jen just said that the party's on Peru Street."

The freshmen girls come and go, year after year. Funny how their ages never change, while I keep growing older. *How does that work*, I wondered? The optimism of these young women remains a constant through the years as well. Driving them, I'm always buoyed by their youthful confidence and vitality.

When I pulled up to the dorm the three girls scurried up to the cab and jammed into the back seat. As usual, they were coatless despite the frigid night air. Hats, of course, are out of the question. I believe I'll see Senator Leahy don a toupée before I witness my first college girl wearing a warm woolen hat. It's a "hair thing," I gather.

"So, where's Peru Street?" Zooey asked as we got underway. "Is it near Loomis?"

"No, not exactly. You girls are headed to the ghetto tonight. Peru isn't what I'd call a student area."

Zooey pivoted in her seat like a basketball point guard. "Jen, what did you get us into here? How exactly do you know this boy who invited us?"

In the rearview I could see that Jen was flustered. "Zooey, it was that guy Shawn from Biology. You know — the kid with the brown hair, parts it kinda in the middle. He said it's going to be, like, an awesome party. That's all I know. Gee, I'm sorry."

"Hey, Zooey," I interjected. "I was just kidding about that 'ghetto' business. Burlington's a safe town. I'm sure it'll be fine. If there's any problem, you just call me and I'll pick you back up in a jiffy."

"What's the matter with you guys?" The third girl had jumped into the fray. "What are we, in high school? We can, like, so take care of ourselves. Quit wimping out."

"You're right, Lanie," Zooey retreated. "I'm over-reacting. We're in college, now. We can handle whatever the night brings. Right, girls?"

We found the number on Peru. The place was one in a series of attached apartments, each with its own street-level front door and short staircase. The exterior siding looked like it was painted white, but that would be merely a guess at this stage of the wear and tear. Two exceedingly sleazy-looking guys were smoking on the steps. When my three attractive, fresh-faced coeds got out of the cab, the guys eyed them like a pair of leopards scoping out a trio of young springbok who had wandered away from their mother at the waterhole. *Well, we'll see,* I thought to myself. *I'm just glad there's three of them.*

The call came 45 minutes later. "Jernigan, come back and get us." It was Zooey and she sounded genuinely distressed. "You were right! We shouldn't be going out during exam week. What were we thinking?"

"Zooey, grab your friends and wait outside. I'm downtown; I won't be five minutes."

When I reached the apartment, the girls were shivering on the sidewalk. A young man — Shawn, perhaps? — was talking to them very intensely, with a lot of suspect hand and head movement. He looked like one of those litigants pleading a dubious case to Judge Judy. To their credit, it looked like the girls were having none of it. As soon as they spotted me, they joined hands and sprinted to the cab.

Diving into the rear seat, Zooey shouted, "Go, go, go!" I hit the gas feeling like the driver of a getaway car. "Omigod, Omigod!" she continued. "How horrible was that?"

"Were we, like, the only females at that party?" Jen said. She was still shivering, and I couldn't tell if it was cold, fear or a combination of the two. "I mean, it was like 50 sketchy guys and us."

I drove and just listened. It was as if they were debriefing, giving testimony as a means of release from the experience. It didn't appear that any of them had suffered serious assault, thank goodness, but they were all shaken up. To my list of the qualities characterizing freshmen girls, I mentally added "naïve."

"I tried dancing with this one guy," Lanie began, clearly in high outrage. "Just, like, you know, to be nice. He wouldn't stop grabbing my ass! It was disgusting. He, like, wouldn't take the hint."

"You are not kidding!" Jen jumped in. "It was like Planet of the Gropers in there! Wait'll I see Shawn again. What a total jerk!"

There was silence in the cab for a moment. Then the three friends spontaneously turned toward each other and began to laugh. It began as chuckles, but quickly progressed to full-blown belly laughter. It was great to see. Nothing's more important than resiliency, I thought, in making a successful life.

"Jernigan," Zooey said, wiping a tear of laughter from her face, "the next time we call you to take us to some random party, you just say 'no,' OK?"

"You got it, Zooey." I replied. "Now when we get back to the dorms, I want to see you all to hit those books!"

Fifty Ways

Lanie is an occasional as opposed to a regular. I consider as regulars my customers who use me at least a few times a month. I hear from Lanie only about every couple of months, and always to go downtown. She lives in one of the outlying condo developments that have taken root throughout Chittenden County suburbia like zebra mussels on the docks of Lake Champlain.

Lanie's a homegirl: Burlington High School, Champlain College and now a dental hygienist at a local dental office. I put her in her early thirties. From conversations, I know she's married and has two young kids. She's a beautiful woman in a wholesome, down-to-earth way. She calls to mind a woman they might cast as a cowgirl on a Nashville Network video, the young wife the country singer has lost through some combination of temptation, stupidity, and hubris, and to whom he's now begging, "Darlin', please take me back; I've seen the light and changed my ways."

It was a weeknight when I picked Lanie up with her sister and two friends. When I bopped the horn, the four of them bunny-hopped out the front door, guffaws aplenty. They were decked out — dressed to maim, if not kill. They bubbled into the taxi, a kinetic collage of sparkling earrings, sparkling laughter and pastel party dresses.

"This is Jernigan, girls," Lanie said as she settled into the front seat. "I told you all about him. He's the best cabbie in town."

The three women in the rear erupted in renewed fits of giggles. There was nothing particularly hilarious in Lanie's introduction of me; it was just the mood of the evening.

One of the friends leaned forward, a long cigarette dangling precariously over my right shoulder. She had stylishly cropped, red-streaked hair. I think I noticed gold glitter mixed in with her blush; her face was so close to mine it was hard to tell. "Well then, Mr. Best-Cabbie-In-Town," she said, "how's it hanging?"

With that zinger, the whole crew began laughing so uproariously it looked as if they were reaching that tipping point where it's almost crying. "I'm gonna pee," Lanie's sister let out between cackles. "I swear I'm gonna pee!"

"No, I *mean* it," Lanie said as the howls gradually subsided to chortles. "This man is a sweetie. He really is." She gazed at me with warm, open eyes.

I like to think of myself as a sweetie, after a sort, but I couldn't tell where she was coming from. I could recall a few discussions with her about relationships; in true cabbie style, I'm always blabbing unsolicited pearls of wisdom to my unfortunate captive audiences. But I couldn't recall anything in the tenor of our past talks to warrant such flattering comments.

"We can't stay out too late, so could you pick us up at 11?" Lanie asked.

"Sure," I replied. "You got my card. If you need to change the time, just call." I then dropped them off at a popular downtown restaurant best known for its pick-up bar.

At half past 10, Lanie called. "We met some really cool guys and we're going to hang with them awhile. Can you come get us at one?" She then gave me the address for one of the new condos on the waterfront. At one, I was parked in front of the address I had been given. After a few minutes, I was considering getting out and knocking on the door when out they paraded. The group now appeared drunker, but less boisterous, almost sullen.

"Well, that was stupid," said the friend with the glittery blush once we were underway. "I can't believe how late this night has gone."

Lanie twisted around in her seat. Apparently, she was the primary moving force behind the waterfront addendum to the evening festivities. She said, "Their apartment was so posh. And they were cool guys, weren't they?"

"Sure, Lanie," her sister shot back. "To you they're all cool guys." Her words dripped with barely contained disdain. "Do you think your husband would enjoy meeting them? How cool would that be?"

Lanie spun back around in the seat. She began tapping on the dashboard with the three middle fingers of her left hand, and I could see her jaw tighten. I imagined this type of repartee with her sister was all too familiar, but tonight she wasn't going to go there.

"So, Jernigan, I wanted to thank you so much for your advice." Lanie's voice was now soft and low. "My husband and I are going to a counselor, and it's really helping. You have a special gift of insight, do you know that?"

A light snow was making it hard to keep track of the car lanes. There were hardly any other vehicles on the road, it being midweek and so late, but still I try to stay in lane. It's my job to drive people safely. It's not organ replacement surgery, but it's what I do and I take it seriously. The thing was, Lanie's buttery words didn't feel right. There was an intimacy that wasn't earned, an assumed connection that bothered me.

"I don't know about that," I said. "If something we talked about helped you out, I'm sure it wasn't any great powers of perception on my part. Still, I'm glad things are going well for you." I straightened up in my seat trying to raise my level of focus.

With two fingers, Lanie lifted an amber ringlet from the side of her face and tucked it behind her ear. She then placed her hand on my right arm which was sitting on the arm rest. She said, "Modesty doesn't suit you real well, do you know that? It's rare that somebody tunes into me the way you do."

The sister's face suddenly appeared between the two of us. "Hey Lanie," she said, her voice musical with mock curiosity. "What the hell are you talking about with this cabdriver? 'Cause, you know, it sounds real interesting."

Just then, thank goodness, we arrived in front of her condo. One of the friends paid the fare, and they all piled out. I hoped they were all staying over at Lanie's place; not one of them was in shape to drive.

Lanie turned and smiled at me as she turned to walk up the driveway. Watching her, an old Paul Simon melody popped into my head, complete with new lyrics — *There must be 50 ways to leave your lover. Just call up your hackie, Jackie; grab a new cab, Ahab; get in the taxi, Maxie . . .*

7

LOST SOULS

Some of our brothers and sisters struggle mightily to find their way in this world, somewhere to fit in, a place that feels like home. To look down with judgment and scorn on such folks is, to me, nearly an unforgivable sin. Because, truly, there but for the grace of God . . .

Two Girls

A small mound of objects was piled up by the side of the bus terminal. There were at least two beat-up suitcases, a cardboard box overflowing with CD's and a cheap-looking CD player, two or three shopping bags of clothing, and what appeared to be a rolled-up mattress stuffed into a lawn-and-leaf size, white plastic bag. This impromptu and temporary structure was crowned by a pudgy teddy bear with sad, black button eyes and a farmer's hat. I couldn't quite tell if the straw hat was permanently affixed to the bear, or if the designers of this edifice had simply deemed the bear noggin a convenient hat rack. The entire tableau evoked an eviction of someone of very meager possessions.

"Hey, Mr. Cabbie, can you take us?"

I turned to look into the faces of two girls who had appeared at my window. Despite the bright sun, the window was tightly shut. It was one of those bitter Burlington January days — close to zero with a relentless wind shrieking off the lake. The first thing that struck me was the insufficiency of the taller girl's jacket. It was a blue windbreaker, more a fall garment, and it's ineffectiveness to the task at hand was evident — the girl wearing it was in a continuous, full-bodied tremble. I rolled down my window to speak.

"Where are you girls going?" I asked.

The shorter one seemed to be in charge and, as such, did the talking. "They said there's a place that, like, helps out teenagers. They told me it's, like, on Pearl Street." Each sentence was enunciated as a question, in the manner of today's young girls. "I remember — it's called Spectator."

"I think it's Spectrum you want," I said. "It's a youth service agency, and it *is* located on Pearl. I think you're right; I bet they could help you out."

"Right on!" she said, and smiled like it was the best news she'd heard in quite a while.

The pile of stuff indeed belonged to them, and the three of us managed to squeeze it all into the vehicle using the entire trunk and most of the front seat. I worked quickly because I really wanted to get the shivering girl into the warm cab; it bothered me to see a kid in that state, so buffeted by the elements.

As the cab wended its way through the clogged downtown streets, the shorter girl was pointing things out. "You see, Diane, that's Church Street. Isn't it totally like I told you? There's a lot of cool kids in this town. You're gonna love it here."

"What brings you guys to Burlington?" I asked.

"Oh, my mom kicked us out. We're from Brattleboro." Her voice was matter-of-fact, neither sad, angry or emotional in any way I could detect. "My sister, Diane, this is her first time up to Burlington. I'm 18, you know. Everyone thinks I'm, like,15. My aunt told me that before long I'll be happy that I look younger than my age, but I think it, like, sucks."

In the rearview mirror I looked at her face, and I would have guessed 13. Her features were tiny, except for the huge, brown eyes which appeared saucer-like under the heavy, black eye make-up. She had long, straight blond hair with a small, woolen beanie hat. She struck me as a human version of a Disney forest creature, maybe a bunny rabbit or a prairie dog. Looking into that face, my paternal instincts kicked into high gear.

"What about school?" I asked. "Have you completed high school?"

"I just got a couple of classes to get my G.E.D. Diane's just in ninth grade. She's only 14."

I glanced over at the other girl, whose demeanor betrayed none of the desperate straits in which she found herself. If anything, Diane appeared even more nonchalant than her older sibling.

The ride to Spectrum took only a few minutes. I pulled into the adjacent parking lot located in the rear of what I still insist on calling the Abernathy building, though the department store's been closed for ages. While her older sister went into the office, Diane and I unloaded their entire worldly possessions, essentially reassembling the pile from the bus terminal.

For a minute, Diane stood there clutching the teddy bear (whose sporty hat was indeed a permanent fixture), the tremble beginning to reemerge. Passersby would have seen a cold, fresh-faced girl holding a bear; they would have had no idea that the child was in free fall. Her sister returned with another teenager, a young man, and she said they said it was OK to bring their stuff into the building. She paid the fare, and I wished them luck. I figured they hadn't been too lucky thus far.

A few days later I ran into a female friend and I related the story of these two girls. I ended the account by mentioning how well they seemed to be navigating their overwhelming life challenges. "Isn't it great," I said, "how resilient young people can be? You'd think these two kids would be falling apart, and yet they demonstrated an amazing degree of emotional equilibrium."

My friend gave me the look I often see on the faces of my acquaintances during certain conversations. It's a look of sweetness and infinite patience, a look that says, "Jernigan, Jernigan, Jernigan . . . just how clueless are you?" Finally, she softly spoke. "What you saw in those two girls had nothing to do with 'emotional equilibrium.' They were probably numb, Jernigan. When you're that completely neglected, that uncared-for, you simply stop feeling anything. That's how you survive."

The instant those words left my friend's mouth, I recognized them as precisely true. Amidst a material bounty the likes of which the world has never before seen, there's so much pain, particularly among so many of the children. For not the first time in my life, I stood aghast at how much I live in a daydream, not unlike the two girls. We have a tacit agreement: They pretend not to feel it, and I'll pretend not to see it.

As I mull it over, now a few weeks down the road, it occurs to me that these sisters have at least two things going for them. First, they have each other. Second, as their place of refuge, they've not gotten off a bus in New York City or Las Vegas, but Burlington — a town that, despite its short-comings, has a heart as big as Camel's Hump and as deep as the big lake.

May a little of that Queen City magic find its way into the life of the two girls, like snowflakes came to Dorothy in the field of poppies, like snow-flakes on a clear, bright January day in Vermont.

Bad Boy

If you were from Burlington and I mentioned the name of Gareth's father, you would recognize it. The old guy is a genuine muck-a-muck, one of the inner circle of (mostly) men who move and shake this town. In bygone years, the press would have dubbed him a Captain of Industry. Maybe the pressure, the burden of expectation which comes with being the son of such a high-powered and successful sire has taken its toll on Gareth. Not really knowing him, though, I couldn't say.

By day, Gareth is a state bureaucrat. Do I know as fact that he secured his relatively cush job through his well-connected family? No, but let's call it a reasonable assumption. By night, he's a drunk, and downtown is his haunt. More nights than not, you can watch him drift from bar to bar like a honeybee in a field of wild flowers. As he absorbs the liquid pollen, his determined gait gradually deteriorates to a barely controlled stumble. He rarely makes it to last call before he's teetering on the curb, hailing a taxi.

He opens the front door and sloshes into the passenger seat. His body mass suggests a blown-up version of the Indian dessert, gulab jamun: a chunk of sponge cake soaked in a fragrant, syrupy liquid. It's common knowledge that the human body is largely composed of water though, of course, we appear as solid entities. This is not quite the case with Gareth. His body appears poached, as if he's undergoing reverse phylogeny and the de-volution has entered the amphibious stage. Before he opens his mouth, I'm hit with a waft of treacly odor, the sick, sweet tang of the truly pickled.

"Hey, man — you know where to go, right?" He mentions his condo unit on Kennedy Drive. "I'm a bad boy. You know that, right? I'm a bad, bad boy."

"Sure, Gareth," I reply. "I know where you live. You saved money for the cab now, did ya?"

More than once I've driven Gareth home only to discover that he's broke, and has to make it into his place (no small endeavor in his condition) to dig out some cash and bring it back out to me — all this only after spending any length of time fishing through each pocket, checking and rechecking. The last time I drove him this little fandango took 25 minutes.

"Oh, I got the money all right, I got the money." He sits up in the seat, furrows his brow and straightens out his pie-eyed, crooked smile. This display is his attempt, I gather, at Upright Citizen.

Though not exactly flooded with confidence, I head towards Kennedy Drive. I have this terrible habit. What do they say? "Fool me once, shame on you; fool me twice, shame on me." I'm way past that, more like I play Charlie Brown to the world's Lucy. I keep thinking, *this time, for sure, she's going to hold the ball.* You'd think by this late date I'd have achieved the seasoned patina of the world-weary, the worldly-wise — something worldly. But no, I just go on believing — despite all evidence to the contrary — that perhaps, the next time, Gareth won't let me down.

"Thank you for the ride," he says. "I really appreciate it."

Oh no, I think, *here we go with the thank you's.* The car, meanwhile, is bumping and grinding through the extended construction site up by the University. The announced completion date of this project is two years off. I'm an avid fan of road-widening — it's actually one of my very favorite things — but it seems the Great Pyramids of Egypt went up quicker, and I'm pretty sure back then they didn't have backhoes.

"Thank you so much," he continues laying it on. "Thanks for the ride. I'm so grateful. You're great, you are just so great."

I don't acknowledge this with a "you're welcome," because I've been through this routine umpteen times with Gareth. He's either crying over the detestable, worthless person he is, or thanking or praising me with an ardor wildly out of proportion to the rather junior favor I am performing, i.e., transporting him home for money. I've tried over the years, but there's no communicating with him, not in any meaningful sense of the word — there's simply no possibility of exchange, give-and-take, meeting-of-the-minds. The guy is lost, and it's heart wrenching to behold.

I pull into the parking space in front of his condo. "Oh Jesus," he says. "I know I got the money here somewhere. I'm such a bad boy."

"Get out of the taxi, Gareth." Tonight, it seems, I've reached my limit.

"What are you talking about?" he shoots back, with a pitiful attempt at indignity. "Why are you being weird? I got the money; I told you I got it here somewhere."

"Just get out," I say, reaching across his body and flipping open the door. He gets out and, with his version of a huff, slams the door.

The next day I drive to the office where I know he works, and I walk up to a customer- service window. I ask, "A guy named Gareth works here, right?"

The older woman behind the counter looks at me askance. "I'll get him for you," she replies.

Gareth walks up to the window and signals me to meet him at a door at the side of the big room. Never before have I seen him sober; it's as if I'm addressing a living being for the first time.

"I drove you home last night." I say. "You owe me 19 bucks, and that includes 10 for the time it's taking me to collect it."

A look of shame passes across his eyes. I can tell he has no recollection of the incident. He pulls out his wallet and hands me a twenty and a ten.

"Keep it man," he says. "I'm really sorry to put you out."

He looks sincere, I can feel it. In that instant, I can see the weight of the pain he carries in his heart.

"OK, thanks," I reply. I pause for a moment before taking leave. "Take care of yourself, Gareth," I add. "I mean, really. Please, get yourself some help." He nods his head, and I turn and walk away.

Extended substance abuse does a number on the human core. I've heard the phrase "soul murder" used in this regard, but I don't buy it. I don't believe the soul can be killed. But it sure as hell can be hijacked and held hostage.

This is the approach to life to which I aspire: We're all in this together, nobody gets left behind. So my question is, what do we do about Gareth?

Night Passenger

It's just past midnight and the moon is a spotlight in a night sky devoid of clouds. I hate full moons because it's true what they say. A rummy, gravelly male voice is on my cellular ordering a cab to an address on a tiny, tucked-away street in the Old North End. The voice is not familiar. *This guy is not a regular*, I think. *Wonder where he got my card?*

I arrive at the street and turn onto it. Though not a dead-end, it's one of those streets you rarely take unless your destination is a home on the street itself. I know I've been down this road before; this is Burlington, and I've been at this a long time. But damned if it doesn't feel like virgin territory.

Between the street lamps and the moon, the light is no worse than a gray afternoon, and I can easily make out the house numbers. I pull up and come to a stop in front of the house the voice specified, and I'm certain I've never seen *this* place before. It's a three-story apartment house with the look of a cellblock. In front are two rectangular dirt patches with not a shrub of grass. The walls are dove-gray concrete cinder blocks, dappled with either a 100 years of grime, or maybe something living, like lichen or black moss.

The heavy front door (perversely painted lime green) opens in slow-motion, and a woman's form comes into view. At first glance, I put her early to mid-thirties, attractive, though in an unfamiliar, vaguely disconcerting manner. She's staring straight ahead as she pauses in the doorway. Her hair is thick and dirty blonde, piled in a large, makeshift bun with helix strands tumbling about her neck and shoulders. Her facial features are small, distinct and delicate: crescent eyes of the darkest brown, and precisely painted, thin magenta lips. She's wearing a charcoal coat of thick cotton matting reminiscent of the outerwear of Chinese peasant women. Three dull, silver bracelets dangle loosely on her left wrist. Her long skirt is the color of ripe wheat, and looks silken, almost shimmery. Multi-laced, jet black boots complete the attire.

As she makes her way down the three front steps, I see she's limping noticeably, using a cane to maintain her balance. Her right leg appears shorter than the left. I can make out the cane more clearly as she approaches the taxi. Her right hand grips the top, which is hooked like a tiger's claw. The shaft is quite thick, I want to say massive, and tapers only slightly towards the bottom, where it terminates in a blackened knob. At first I think the body of the cane is scratched up but, in the next moment, it looks like intricate carvings of animals or people. Just as quickly, it returns to haphazard scratches. Is it the moonlight, or what?

She opens the car's front door, and my reaction to her physical presence is immediate and visceral. Some part of me engages far deeper, way below the cerebral cortex. A feeling enshrouds my body, and a word fills every square inch of the taxi's interior space, as if the vehicle had just plunged into the lake. The word is "death."

I have never before had a bodily experience of such aberrant power, not even remotely, not even close. Through the years, I have developed the ability to interact with cokeheads, alcoholics, crazy people, nasty frat boys, homeless indigents — the full gamut of humanity — all without losing my sense of self, without being pulled into the other's experiential state. I take pride in this, the maintenance of clear professional boundaries. In a flash, this woman has blown down these walls. Meanwhile, one second has elapsed.

After first carefully placing her cane into the vehicle, she then drops herself into the front seat with just a little angling awkwardness. "Go," she says, still staring straight ahead.

Her voice, in that single word, concentrated and elevated my already sky high feeling of dread. It was flat, atonal, yet paradoxically resonant and rich. Was it loud or soft? I can't say if she had whispered or bellowed. All that is eerie enough, but bush league bizarreness compared to this aspect: From where did the voice emanate? I saw her lips move, but it was like watching a ventriloquist's puppet. Inexplicably (to say the least), the sound was disembodied.

The Jernigan who is still being the cabdriver sputters out, "Could you, like, be a tad more specific?" I have a steadfast policy: give me the final destination, not "left, right, straight, go, turn."

"Colchester Village," she replies.

Though not perfect, that's sufficiently specific to get the taxi in drive. Down the hill, past the tower and grave of Ethan Allen, over the Winooski

Bridge, up the hill, past Exit 16, and we enter the long drop through Sunny Hollow.

Not a word is exchanged. The moon is burning. Logically, of course, it's the sun that burns; the moon is but reflective. But tonight the moon seems to have an interior light source, a generator independent of the sun. I truly wish this wasn't so, because it's just one more uncanny thing I'm forced to cope with, but tonight it is.

At the nadir of the glen, a doe suddenly appears on the shoulder of the road. As we zoom towards her, her head turns to face us. For an instant, the animal's eyes light up like blood-red embers and, in the next moment, she leaps into the brush, vanishing into the verdured safety. *OK*, I think, scrambling to steady my attention, *did that really happen?*

I slowly turn to peer at my customer, an action I have been studiously avoiding until now. She's still staring straight ahead. Under normal circumstances — a state of being for which I would, at this moment, trade my left little toe — the obvious question is, "Did you just see what I just saw?" Not tonight, however. Not with this person, not at this moment. I am scared beyond speech; I am full-fledged freaking out, and I have no idea how to shake it.

Nothing outwardly can explain this fear. I am simply driving a customer from one place to another, as I do dozens of times a week, thousands of times a year. What on earth is going on?

Then it dawns on me. I am in the presence of a witch. Not a good witch, either. Not Glinda. No, this is the variety upon which houses occasionally drop, if you're lucky.

What the *hell* am I thinking? Have I lost every single one of my marbles? Not that I don't believe in ethereal reality — inner planes of existence, the cosmic, the astral. In theory, I subscribe to the existence of incorporeal beings of one sort or another. The twist is, I've never personally had a tête-à-tête with any *Beetlejuice*-type characters. Until now, anyway.

Turning onto 2A at the Spanked Puppy tavern, she signals with a single flick of her finger to take a left, and now we're heading north into that interregnum where Colchester, Essex and Milton blend together in a no-man's land. We're beyond the street lights, the road is dirt, the houses far and few between, and fear — stomach-gripping, stark-raving fear — has seized my psyche. I have visions of my imminent demise: it will be slow, and it will be gruesome. I find myself praying to God, with moving lips and all, for my deliverance.

Time has ceased. The passing trees are purple, the houses now non-existent. We've made a few turns; I've lost count. I have absolutely no idea where we are, but does it matter, really? Perhaps we're still in Vermont, my beloved adopted state. Perhaps we're still on the earth plane, and that would be keen. I am aboard the Titanic; no need to maintain an accurate log when the outcome is pre-ordained.

Finally, we turn up a steep, ragged driveway. My shocks can't take it. My head is bouncing around like a bobble-head doll; it feels like it's big and jiggling ludicrously on a spring. This actually begins to feel pleasant, probably because, at his point, I'm slightly delirious.

After about a quarter-mile — or was it 20 miles? — the road spills out into a large, crater-filled parking area. Off to one side sits a beat-up house trailer with a single burning candle visible through a translucent window. This is so beyond spooky; like spooky exists in pre-school, and I've somehow found myself in the Harvard Doctoral Program for Advanced Studies in Sheer Terror.

My customer turns to pay and, as she hands me the money, she looks at me for the first, and God-willing, last time. The crescent brown eyes are saucer wide, locked on me dead-on, yet it feels as if she's looking through me, at someone standing two feet behind me. I have the sensation of my soul being cooked. But even more horrifically poignant, it feels like there's nobody home in those eyes. Just like the voice, there's a pervasive aura of disembodiment.

Please, I mouth these words. *Let it be quick and painless.*

But nothing happens. The second the woman steps out of the cab and closes the door behind her, I spin the vehicle around and hightail it down the driveway, like I am a bat, and yes, this is hell. My heart is pounding as I somehow find my way back to Route 7, and head south — back to life, back to reality.

This fare, my strangest in all my years of hacking, took place a few years ago, just before Halloween as I now think about it. A major case of residual willies clung to me for a few days. Then, like the shock response to a traumatic injury, I must have blocked the entire incident from my memory.

It came back to me this week. Voilà *— just like that. If the whole thing sounds dream-like, and not just a little crazy — well, it was. As a matter of fact, I'm not going to ever mention it again. Sometimes, I believe, you ignore the old folk adages at your peril: Speak of the devil . . .*

Lost Lambs and GMC Vans

I had first seen the young woman earlier that afternoon walking along Pine Street near the Burlington bus terminal. I tend to notice people on the sidewalk, because anyone on foot is a potential taxi fare. So I keep my eyes open.

She had been heading in the direction of Main Street with a substantial backpack in tow — big, rectangular, frayed and tan. Judging from the bulk of it, I imagined she was carrying all her worldly possessions on her back. Her worn clothes suggested that she was not a middle-class kid out on a lark with a handy credit card if things got dicey. You can never tell for sure, but I had a strong sense this person was likely living on the wings of fate, out on the edge.

It was close to midnight when this same young woman approached my taxi. I rolled down my window and she said, "I'm supposed to meet a guy with a van in front of Shaw's on — I think he said, 'Shelburne Street.' Also, he has the money for the taxi when we get there. Is that OK?"

"Yeah, Shaw's on Shelburne Road. Let's throw that backpack in the rear seat, and you can sit in the front with me."

"What about the money part?"

"It's fine," I replied. "You just pay me when we get there. That'll work."

In most situations I'll decline a proposal with such an iffy financial outlook. But she wasn't going too far and, beyond that, like many lawyers (or at least the decent ones), I'm OK with doing some *pro bono* work now and then, if that's what it comes down to.

We turned onto St. Paul Street, heading to Route 7. The girl sat next to me, her hands folded on her lap, somehow fresh-faced and dirty at the same time. I don't mean dirty like a hustler, sleazy and unclean, but literally adorned with the sheen of road dust.

"What brings you through town?" I asked.

"I heard that this was a good place," she replied. "You know — like there's good people here. Do you think so?"

"Well, I've done my share of traveling back in the day, and my experience is that there's good people everywhere."

She chuckled and pulled her long dark hair behind her ears, looping it into a pony tail with a thick, red rubber band. "Well, I don't know about *that*," she said.

I smiled inwardly and thought, *there's a real sweetness about this girl.* She then said, "Hey, what's your name, dude?"

"My name's Jernigan."

"Really?"

"Yup. I mean, why would I make up a name? It's not like I'm a stripper or something. What's yours?"

"My name is Janice."

"Well, good to meetcha Janice," I said, and took the left into the Shaw's shopping center. Sure enough, there was a GMC van with its dim lights on, sitting in the shadows at the far end of the parking lot. We pulled alongside it and eased to a stop. Janice instructed, "He said to honk."

I lightly tapped the horn, and a hulking man pushed open the two back doors of the van and stepped out. He wore black jeans and no shirt or shoes. If he was riding a skateboard, it occurred to me, with an unleashed pit bull, he would be in violation of every single posted rule on the Church Street Marketplace. Well, maybe he'd have to spit a few times, as well. His left bicep was wrapped in what looked like Saran Wrap. He walked around to the passenger side of the cab just as my customer was getting out.

"It's Janice, right?" he said. "Take a look at this tattoo I told ya I was getting."

"Sure, dude."

He carefully rolled down the plastic film to reveal a gold and crimson tiger. The colors were startlingly vivid; the big cat looked almost liquid. Janice said, "Nice ink."

"You think so?" the guy said with a leer in his voice. He looked at least 15 years older than Janice. He strode around to me and paid the fare without making eye contact. "C'mon inside the van," he continued talking to Janice. "I got another tat to show you."

"Let me grab my pack," she said.

"Right on," he said, climbing back into his vehicle.

Janice opened the rear door of my cab and lifted out her backpack. She then stuck her head back through the door and asked, "You think this guy's a good person?"

No, Janice, I don't think so, was the answer that popped into my brain. But I suppressed that and said, "How can I say? I've just met him for two minutes. Just take care of yourself, whatever happens."

The saddest look washed over her face. For travelers on the wings of fate, unfortunately, mercy can be hard to come by.

"I hope he doesn't hurt me," she said, and closed the door.

That remark, wish — whatever — hit me like a kick in the stomach. I couldn't bear to contemplate exactly what she meant by it. My mind flashed on a bumper sticker I've been seeing a lot lately: "All who wander are not lost."

True enough, I thought. *But some are.*

The Boxer

All us cabbies know Frankie because he's always taking cabs. It's usually at night, and often amidst a minor crisis. "Well, she kicked me out again," or "Could you get me out to the Trackside before 11? There's a guy there owes me 50 bucks; I been trying to catch up with him for a month." If it's not one thing it's another.

In my experience, Frankie generally doesn't have the cash to pay for a taxi, or it's one of those when-we-get-there-somebody-will-be-waiting-with-the-money scenarios. For most cabbies, that's a classic non-starter, because — wouldn't you know? — for some reason, the person with the money never seems to materialize at the other end. In any event, lack of capital does nothing to deter Frankie's taxi habit, and he always manages to find a driver to take him. As I said, he's local, he's known, and that qualifies him for a taxi, money or not. I do my best to accommodate him because of who he is and the stories he has to tell. Like, for instance . . .

It was a slow, late May day with the students gone and the summer tourist season not yet underway, so I was more amenable than usual when Frankie hailed from a downtown street corner and outlined a proposed trip to Williston. "I got to pick up a check, and then back to Burlington to cash it at a local bank." I listened and estimated the odds of this ultimately resulting in a paying fare: fifty-fifty. But, as I said, nothing was doing — beyond a little gas, what did I have to lose?

"Sure, Frankie," I said. "Let's go."

Frankie smiled with relief and took a seat beside me. He's a small man with a round head and a shock of dirty brown hair. His arms are strikingly muscular for a man well into his sixties, and his hands and fingers exude concentrated power, like he could be capable of the Superman bended-rod routine. I admire his ears: not overly large, but beautifully shaped with long, detached Buddha-style earlobes.

Perhaps it's odd to speak of ears, but to me it's amazing that his are in such unmarred condition. In his early adulthood — and that would encompass the mid-'50s through the late '60s — Frankie worked as a professional boxer, perhaps the most accomplished fighter ever to emerge from Vermont.

I've never gone on the Internet to verify the various details of his career, but Frankie's told me a lot. Apparently, at various points, he claimed the state title in three different classes: fly, bantam and lightweight. In the greater world of boxing, he was never nationally ranked but was considered a solid journeyman. At times he fought contenders, but never for the title itself. His career record was 147-64. Of the wins, 27 were by knock-out. He claims never to have been knocked out himself.

"Nobody ever knocked me out," he has told me more than once. "Just like Jake LaMotta, I never saw the black lights." (In the poetic language of pugilism, he was referring to the "black lights" of unconsciousness.)

Heading out Route 2 to Williston, Frankie was trying to assure me that the check was "definitely" in his friend's car, and that is was a "lock" I'd be paid for this fare. This was a discussion in which I had no interest, so I quickly switched it to boxing, a subject I find endlessly compelling. I boxed a little as a kid, but lacked the talent, stamina, heart and discipline required to advance beyond the most neophyte levels.

"Frankie," I said, "tell me about your best fight. Which bout was the highlight of your career?"

"Jesus," he replied. "That's an easy call. It was the fight in Lewiston, Maine. Cassius Clay was fighting Sonny Liston on the rematch, and I fought on the undercard. This was just before Clay changed to the Muslim name, Muhammad Ali."

We pulled into at a large factory parking lot in Williston where Frankie's check was supposedly ensconced in the glove compartment of a friend's pickup. Before he got out, I said, "You fought on the same card with Muhammad Ali? That's fantastic. Didja get to meet him? What did you think of his boxing?"

"He was the smartest fighter I ever seen," he said. "He changed his style depending on his opponent's strengths and weaknesses, which is the key to being a winning fighter. I shook his hand that day, and he told me, 'Hey, you little frogman; you go knock him out tonight.'"

Frankie, of French-Canadian heritage, had the boxing moniker the "French Frog." In the ethnically-charged milieu of professional boxing, it was a name he wore with pride.

While Frankie went looking for his check, I pondered that moment so long ago in Maine. What an honor, to receive the personal benediction of the man himself, Muhammad Ali.

Momentarily, my customer returned check in hand. I thought, *will wonders never cease?* We headed back downtown to his bank to cash the check. Frankie has held a number of custodial and handyman jobs since his retirement from the ring. I gather there have been situations where the possibility existed of decent full-time employment with benefits, but personal problems always cropped up and things fell apart.

"Tell me more about the Lewiston match," I said. "Who'd you fight? Who won? I'd love to hear the details."

"I remember it like it happened last week," he began. "I was fighting lightweight, a fighter out of Chicago, a colored guy named Collie Branch. The early rounds were brutal because we fought so alike, our styles I mean. I had this series of punches that always worked for me. Right-hand jab to the left rib cage, left-hand to the right. The second punch always made the guy drop his right arm in pain, and then I'd follow with a solid right uppercut to the jaw. Hey, I'm saying three punches, but they happened in a split second." He then said, "Whap, whap, whap," clapping three times to demonstrate the concept. "I must have dropped a dozen guys with that three-punch combo, but this guy Collie, he would have none of it.

"We fought hard, equal like I said, round after round. My corner man, Sol Linowitz, told me Collie was ahead on points, but how did he know? He was just trying to keep me aggressive. Then, in the final round — the ninth — we was both pouring it on and, at the same instant, we both leaned in, dropped and threw the right to the head."

As Frankie was telling this story, he was simultaneously acting out every move right in his car seat. I was having a hard time keeping my eyes on the road because I didn't want to miss any of the action.

"Bam! We both hit the canvas. The crowd was going nuts — they loved it! I picked up the count at three, and got to my feet at six. Collie lay there dead to the world, but somehow staggered up at the nine count. I hardly remember the rest of the round but, at the bell, Collie wrapped his arms around me and yelled in my ear over the crowd roar, 'Hey Frenchie, you all right man!

"Back in the dressing room, Solly came in to congratulate me. I didn't even know I won! Anyway, that was my greatest fight, and the closest I ever came to getting knocked out — that six-count from Collie Branch's right hook."

We arrived at the bank, but they wouldn't cash his check because he didn't have his I.D. with him. Maybe all those years in the fight game, the thousands of blows, had taken their toll. They used to call it "punch drunk"; really, it's hard to tell. For my part, I was neither surprised nor annoyed.

"Next time you see me, Frankie. You just give me the money then."

Frankie looked back at me with smiling, sad round eyes. I noticed two crescent bands of dark, built-up skin where the cheekbones meet the eye sockets. Scar tissue.

Is boxing inhumane, not befitting our civilized society? Mahatma Gandhi was once asked what he thought of Western civilization. "I think it would be a good idea," he replied.

Frankie went into the ring more than 200 times. He went with his warrior heart and spirit. If he needs a taxi ride now and then, I'll give him one.

Steel Plate Your Heart

"Gosh almighty," Irene said with a smile as she climbed into the front seat of my taxi. "It's still so cold out there!" My regular bus terminal customer was carrying a small knapsack and wearing her one winter coat — a tan sheepskin with fluffy white on all the edges. It looked well-worn, but still clean and serviceable.

I smiled back her. "Well, we're only a week away from spring." I considered this astute observation for a moment and added, "Not that that means a whole heckuva lot, of course."

I backed up the vehicle and swung out onto Pine Street, Irene sitting next to me beaming. Why she always seems so cheerful, I couldn't say. The little bit I know about her points to a hardscrabble life, always on the move from one substandard apartment to another. On earlier trips, I've gotten the impression that her romantic life has been as unstable as her domicile.

"Jeez, Irene, I didn't even ask. Are you going down to that trailer in Shelburne?"

"Yup, I sure am. I'm lucky I have good friends to help me out, 'cause it's wicked hard to find a decent place in Burlington."

Irene raised her hand up to brush a cascade of blonde hair away from her face. She's an attractive woman, I noticed, not for the first time, but with a hardness to her features, an innate toughness. I couldn't tell if she was hanging on by a thread — just about to break — or whether she'd lived so chaotically for so long that she'd somehow made peace with it. For me, such a volatile, touch-and-go lifestyle would be intolerable. Not that I'm living in the Trump Towers with room service, but at least I have the same, steady roof over my head every night.

"I just couldn't stay in Montpelier," she continued. "The heat hardly worked in that apartment, and the frickin' landlord wouldn't do diddly squat to fix it."

Irene was crashing at a friend's trailer on Shelburne Road, just south of the bowling alley. Most people wouldn't speak of trailer parks and Shelburne — one of the wealthiest towns in the state — in the same breath. But this one's been around for years, tucked discretely off Route 7 and barely visible from the road.

As we cruised passed the Price Chopper, Whitney Houston came on the radio singing, "I Will Always Love You." Irene laughed and said, "I kinda liked this song when it first came out, but then they played it to death."

"Yeah, I know what you mean. Hey, didja know that it was written by Dolly Parton?"

"No — get on!"

"I'm not kidding. Dolly's a great songwriter. If you can look past all that make-up, the huge hair, the flashy clothes, she's a great country singer. I don't know about you, but when I listen to her I can really hear the bluegrass coming through. Dolly's got soul, doncha think?"

"Oh, God, yes. She's great. You gotta love Dolly Parton."

We rolled along listening to Whitney belting out Dolly's tale of loss and forgiveness. If the story's true, this song was Dolly's poignant good-bye to Porter Wagoner, her long-time singing partner. Shelburne Road, it occurred to me, is a perfect thoroughfare for a certain strain of country music, what with all the cheap motels, fast food joints and dislocated people.

"You're a Vermonter, aren't you, Irene? What town did you grow up in?"

"I grew up in Barre, so I guess maybe I'm a Vermonter. My father was a granite cutter. A couple of my uncles, too. My dad died when I was a girl, but I still got his boots. They're beat up something awful, but covering the toes they still got these steel plates like you wouldn't believe. Supposed to protect you if one of the stones gets loose and drops on your feet." Irene paused and gently shook her head. "But like Dad used to say, 'Don't count on it.'"

A few construction crew workers were out by the side of the road, signaling the restart of the Shelburne Road widening project. Despite the wintry weather, I took this as a hopeful sign of spring. When we came up on Champlain Lanes, Irene had me pull into the big parking to drop her off.

She paid me the fare and threw in a fat tip, as she always does. It kills me when someone of such limited funds lays a big tip on me. Don't get me wrong — I'm utterly appreciative of a good tip, no matter the source. But when it comes from someone like Irene, it warms my heart along with my pocket.

"Hey, Irene," I said, "Did your dad ever tell you any cool stories about the boots?"

"Nope, not really," she replied, smiling as brightly as ever. "You know what, though? I put 'em on sometimes."

"Really?"

"Sounds weird, huh?" Irene stepped out of the cab, and just before she closed the door she added, "It makes me feel safe."

8

CURBSIDE ATTRACTIONS

Sometimes the action occurs outside the confines of the taxi, and cruising the streets offers me a front-row vantage seat.

Fearless Cabbie Saves the Day!

The intersection of St. Paul and Main Streets has been a taxi staging area for as long as cabs have rolled in the Queen City. Back in the day, I'm told, the entire north side of Main, from St. Paul to Church Street, was one continuous cabstand. Throughout the day, buses would pull in and out of Vermont Transit — currently home to the "Hempest" clothing store (I guess when the garments wear out, you can grind them up and smoke them) — and the taxi line moved in a steady flow. According to the one remaining old-timer who goes back that far, there was always a brisk business transporting soldiers out to Fort Ethan Allen before it was decommissioned in the '50s.

When I got into hacking around 1980, Vermont Transit was still there, along with an old-fashioned newspaper-and-candy store next door . . .

It's a lazy summer afternoon, not much business, and I'm lingering at the cabstand. *What the heck,* I say to myself — *time to get a paper. Something to break the tedium.* So I mosey across the street, as I've done a thousand times before, and approach the door of the newsstand. But just before I enter, I see something through the storefront window that freezes me in my tracks.

The store clerk is standing behind the counter, arms pointing to the ceiling, his face locked in fear. On the customer side of the counter, a guy with a black kerchief covering his face is aiming a revolver at the clerk's torso.

"Holy craaaaaap!" rushes through my brain. "Holy friggin' crap!"

Now my back is plastered to the wall adjacent to the store. Quaking in my sneakers, I edge back to the window and sneak a tiny peak. No change in the scenario. I basically freak out, run like a crazy person across the street, and cower behind my rear fender. Heightening the surrealism of the moment, people are milling about here and there on the sidewalks, totally oblivious.

I crawl into my cab and get on the car phone — this was before cell phones — and call 911.

"The newsstand by the bus is getting robbed!" I manage to spit out through the fear and adrenaline. "For God's sake — call the cops!"

"Sir, we *are* the cops," an amazingly calm female voice replies. "Number 14 — what's your 10/20?"

I can make out a garbled radio voice. The dispatcher continues, "Shoot over to the newsstand next to Vermont Transit. Robbery in progress." Again, I hear a crackly radio response, something like "10/4."

"Okay, sir, where are you right now?"

"I'm sitting in my cab across the street."

"All right. Don't do anything, a cruiser is on the way. Thanks for calling."

Not more than 20 seconds later, a police cruiser squeals to a stop in front of the bus station. It's blue lights are flashing, but there's no siren. Two police officers leap out, guns drawn and pressed against their thighs, and they edge their way along the wall towards the scene of the crime. Just then I notice a couple on the sidewalk about to cross St. Paul Street.

"Get down!" I yell through my passenger window. I point frantically across the street. "The cops are about to bust up a robbery going down at the newsstand!"

"Holy crap!" the guy says.

"That's what *I* thought!" I reply, and the two people duck behind my cab to watch along with me.

The policemen get to the door and, executing that quick pivoting motion I've seen on endless police shows, they enter the premises. My heart is thumping in my chest. If things are going to get bad, now's the time.

Ten seconds pass and nothing happens. I can't see into the store from my vantage point, but I don't hear anything, certainly no gunshots. Now 20 seconds, and now a minute. Nothing. I can't stand it, and I call back to the couple crouching behind me, "I'm going in." I don't know who the hell I think I am — John Wayne? Angie Dickinson?

I jog across the street, entirely devoid of a plan. I don't know what I'm thinking, or even if I *am* thinking. I'm probably operating out of the pre-mammal brain, behind the cerebral cortex.

I hit the wall, execute the Charlie's Angels spin maneuver — God knows why, as of course I'm unarmed — and the next thing I know I'm in the store.

Down the hill we drove. Bowser sat next to me chatting away, clearly digging his first trip to Vermont. Then, as the van approached downtown, the thought struck me — a new club had recently replaced the old Hunt's nightclub on the corner of Pine Street.

"Bowser, check this out," I said, pointing to the left. "They named this new dance club after you guys. Ain't that great?"

Bowser and the rest of the boys turned in unison just as we passed the old armory building. The sign jutting out from above the front door read, "Sha Na Na's."

Unexpected reaction. I was anticipating, I suppose, an appreciative chuckle. What I got was more along the lines of a startled pit bull.

"What the . . . !" (Expletive deleted. Expletive deleted. Expletive, expletive; deleted, deleted.) "Ralphie, *Ralphie*!"

Initial shock dissipated, Bowser spun in his seat to address one of the guys in the back, presumably their manager. "Ralphie, do we know about this? More to the point, are we getting *paid* for this?"

"Beats me, man," Ralphie answered sheepishly. "First I've heard about it, anyhow."

"That's just what I thought," said Bowser. "OK, we get to the hotel, first thing we get on the line to Woodstein. We sic him on this joker."

Bowser paused for a moment and shifted forward in his seat. He then got this scary grin across his bulbous lips, and resumed speaking.

"He'll love to hear about this one. Woodstein lives for this kind of crap. Inter-fuckin-rogatories, depositions, injunctions — this club guy won't know *what* hit his ass!"

Two weeks later, cruising down Main Street, I noticed that the sign in front of the club had been oh-so-slightly altered. It now read, "Sh' Na Na's." A subtle change, but the first "A" had clearly been excised and replaced by an apostrophe.

So now, dear readers, you know the solution to the puzzle, "Who took the "Sha" out of Sha Na Na's?" The answer: None other than Sha Na Na.

THIS PAGE IS OUT OF ORDER
(SORRY 'BOUT THAT)
– JERNIGAN
↓

The cops are standing by the counter, eating donuts (what else?) while they chat and chuckle with the masked gunman. The clerk is now seated, soda in hand, looking for all the world like he's at a particularly convivial cocktail party. My brain is, at this point, on the fritz. Then I glance to the far side of the store and see two video cameras set up on tripods.

The counter guy notices me and my dopey expression. "Hey, are you the guy who called the cops?" he asks, obviously, though not very effectively, stifling his laughter. "We're filming a commercial. I guess we're doing a good job!"

With that the whole room cracks up. They're not laughing *with* me; they are laughing *at* me. And who can blame them?

"Ho, ho, ho," I join in, attempting to find some way through the utter embarrassment of the situation.

"This is hilarious, just hilarious," I babble on, obvious as I am ridiculous. Then, backing up and nodding my head like a bobble-head doll, I slink out of the store.

The Sha-nectomy or, Who Took the "Sha" Out of Sha Na Na's?

What is it they say about the '80s? If you lived through them, you probably wish you didn't remember. Actually, "they" don't say that; I just made it up. It's a tad harsh, but there's a reason it's been dubbed the Decade of Excess. The '80s were a time of the broad gesture and, as a culture, we did grow more than slightly infatuated with the material aspect of life. Through the cloudy mists of time, I gaze back and remember. Yes, I see myself driving a taxi then as well . . .

In the mid-'80s, the Radisson Hotel was the venue for one of the outsized society events of the era. Two local, hugely successful entrepreneurs were tying the knot, and money, as they say, was no object. The bride and groom were both well-known, well-thought of members of the business community, and their Radisson nuptials were, at the time, a Big Deal.

Personally, I enjoyed no personal connection to such lofty social circles; as usual, it was the transportation factor that placed me in the picture. Throughout the '80s, I operated vans, designed for the transport of small groups. For the reception, the couple had hired the pretend '50s group, Sha Na Na. The band had enjoyed enormous popularity in the '70s, and at one point hosted an eponymous TV series. Though their fame had long-since crested, it was still big potatoes to have Sha Na Na as your wedding band (and hugely expensive, no doubt.) A truck would be hauling the band's equipment up to Burlington. I was engaged to pick up the band members themselves at the airport and drive them to the hotel. Cool!

As I now recall my ride that day with the Sha Na Nites, I have difficulty picturing them. This is because, both musically and visually, I've got them hopelessly confused with the Village People. I do, however, crisply remember the lead singer, the one so demurely known as "Bowser." He was rail thin, with a mouth size rivaling that of Julia Roberts. Two or three quarts of Quaker State, or so it seemed, oozed through his thick, wavy hair. Minus the 10W-40, he looked a lot like Steve Tyler of Aerosmith.

Building a Better Egg Cream

I spent the first 20 years of my life in New York City — Brooklyn, to be precise — and during the last two of those years, I drove a yellow checker taxi in Manhattan. When I share this bit of personal history with someone, the response is invariably some variation of, "Moving up here must have been quite the change." To which I come back with, "Well, I guess maybe" — that phrase being the *ne plus ultra* of emphatic Vermont affirmations. I would say that I took to Vermont like a duck to water, but allusions to aquatic life don't nearly capture the heartfelt relief with which I embraced my new home. "Like a lover" comes closer.

I've rarely look back; my nostalgia for my Big Apple roots is underwhelming. I don't miss the dirty snow on dirty streets; I don't miss the clogged roads; I don't miss the screaming people, screeching cars. But there is one thing I have missed, and that thing is the sweet and creamy, fizzy and chocolaty, improbably named, quintessential NYC fountain drink: the egg cream.

The day of the great New York cafeteria was already on the wane by the mid-'70s. A few still held on: DuBrow's in Brooklyn; the inimitable Horn & Hardhart in Manhattan with its sandwiches behind the coin-operated little windows so captivating to generations of children; and the majestic Bellmore, which took up almost an entire city block on Park Avenue South, just down the road from the Taxi Drivers Union headquarters.

The Bellmore was the preferred meal stop for half a century of NYC cabbies. The entire street in front of the cafeteria was reserved as one extended taxi stand. Early in my hacking career, a veteran cabbie told me about the place and I duly adopted it as my own. Along with a vast array of sandwiches, hot plates, side dishes, desserts, soups — you name it — the Bellmore featured a soda fountain which served up a classic egg cream.

You take a large glass. First, you put in two fingers of chocolate syrup — U-Bet or Chico were the local favorite brands, and the preferred choice of the cognoscenti back in the day. You then add an equal plash of milk. (A plash being a gentle splash.) You next fill 'er up with pure, 100% NYC seltzer, stirring all the way with a long spoon. If you got it right, you're looking at a dark brown quaff topped off by a white cloud head. At the Bellmore, they got it right every time, and many was the driving shift I made my way over to Park Avenue South for this potent reviver.

Now I'm up here in Vermont pushing the hack, and I'm missing the egg cream, when one night it occurs to me: *Perhaps I can bring the mountain to Mohammed?*

Like the scientists of the Manhattan Project, I needed my Los Alamos. What would be the most promising venue for the development and launch of the Queen City egg cream? I settled on the Vermont Pub & Brewery, a popular and easily-accessible downtown eatery with a coterie of friendly and amenable bartenders.

It was a relaxed Sunday evening when I sidled up to the bar and caught the bartender's eye. "What can I get you tonight?" the woman asked me. She had dark, brown eyes, long black hair tied back in attractive, loose braids, and she wore a black apron folded down to waist level. Her eager smile had customer service written all over it; I knew this was my best shot.

There was no way to ease into this, so I took the plunge. I asked, "Could you make me a nice, frothy egg cream?"

She didn't blink, which I took as a good omen. "That was an egg cream, you said?"

"Uh-huh," I replied. "An egg cream."

"Okay, you got me. But just tell me how and I'll make it."

I'm lousy at conveying coherent instructions, but I did my best. The bartender absorbed it attentively. "All right — milk, chocolate syrup, seltzer; we can do that. But where does the egg come in?"

"It doesn't."

"So why is it called an 'egg' cream?" she asked, with unassailable logic.

"That's a great question, and one I'm afraid I can't help you with. And for that matter, don't bother to ask about the cream either. I'm sure there's some ancient New York explanation lost in the mists of time." Now I was on a roll. "It probably goes back to Peter Stuyvesant, or those Indians who sold Manhattan for 11 bucks."

Like most people, I find my own sense of humor hilarious, though by now I've lived long enough to know better. Still, it was nice to see her taking in my doltish history lesson with patience, if not actual interest.

"Well, screw it then," she said gamely. "An egg cream it is, and an egg cream I'll make for you."

She dug up the ingredients, mixed them up, and presented me the glass. I took a swig and — ahh! — it was good. It's surprisingly easy to screw up an egg cream, and for her first attempt, this was marvy. I told her so and left a big tip.

It's now been a few months, and I think by now most of the Pub & Brewery bartenders are egg cream certified. Once in a while, there will be a critical error, as in a recent visit when they made the darn thing with about 50% syrup, 25% milk and 25% seltzer. Junkie that I am, I downed it anyway and lapsed into a sugar coma for about three hours. But, by and large, they're getting it right; not quite the Bellmore, but close enough.

In a spritz and a stir, the final remnant of my attachment to New York City has thus been extinguished.

Surfin' Safari

A streak of faded blue flashes by my driver's window as I dawdle at the Main Street taxi stand. What *was* that? It's a skateboarder crouched low, arms out like an umpire making the safe call, arms out like wings in flight, a condor buzzing the asphalt.

At the intersection of St. Paul, Main Street angles steeper for the final three-block stretch to the lake, and now at car-like speed, the skateboarder takes the line down the center, slicing and dicing the yellow ribbon like some master Japanese chef. I watch him grow smaller, a bobbing blue blur, now passing Champlain Street and spinning to a stop at Battery. I'm jealous.

When I was a kid, skateboarding was in its infancy. Back then, we called it "sidewalk surfing." The technology was primitive: the metal ball bearing wheels were removed from old-fashioned street skates and simply bolted onto an oval-cut piece of wood. The performance of these early boards offered almost no "give," nothing like what guitarists call — in reference to the easy stretch of strings on a well-made guitar — "good action."

The various street hazards, from potholes to broken glass to pedestrians, could stop you dead in your tracks. Or rather, the skateboard would stop and you would keep going, all in accordance with the heartless laws of physics. The resulting skin abrasions we dubbed "road rash." Modern day boards, on the other hand, have wheel mechanisms made from plastic composites — "trucks" in boarder lingo — which allow the rider a degree of maneuvering flexibility we old-timers could only dream about.

What is it about these teenage boys, and the few daring girls, that evoke such animosity in a certain vocal segment of the adult population? Is it the baggy pants, the sullen stares? So much of teenage activity is seen as a "problem to be solved." They take up too much space on Church Street; they're too loud; everything about them is offensive — their dress, tattoos, jewelry, hair, music. My God — the tourists will be frightened!

I love the skateboarders. I dig their style, their attitude, but above all, I admire their bravura. It hurts to hit concrete, and like any of the "sliding" sports — skiing, surfing, ice skating — you only learn by trying and falling. Yowch!

Last week, I watched a band of a half-dozen veteran boarders attack the steps of the old Hotel Vermont, now known as the Vermont House. I say "veteran" because they appeared to be about 16 or 17, and most of the boys leave off this endeavor by their mid-teens.

Street boarders search out buildings with unique and challenging street architecture, such as multi-leveled concrete steps and walls. The superior riders have the ability to leap onto these features and ride 'em for a few glorious seconds before slamming back down to sidewalk level. The Vermont House is particularly enticing due to the long ramp on the east side which brings you up to a raised entrance. The skateboarders, of course, do not take the ramp to enter the building; they continue the few additional yards west to where the stoop ends at four descending, gray steps.

One by one, the boarders took off from the sidewalk in front of the Flynn Theater, quickly accelerated via a kicking foot motion in conjunction with the gravity of the downgrade. They hit the Vermont House ramp like Evel Kneivel at the Grand Canyon, shooting across the short entranceway like a B-24 taking off from an aircraft carrier on the Midway — Tora! Tora! Tora! — and then flew off the top step into the wild blue yonder.

Successfully landing a skateboard from this height and speed is a challenge requiring a great deal of experience and dexterity. That evening, in a rattling display of raw courage, these aviators were attempting a 360-degree rotation before they touched down. One after another, they splashed onto the unforgiving concrete — crash, burn, wipe-out. The attempts went on for 15 minutes as they limped back up to the Flynn and tried again and again. The never-say-die attitude was inspiring; I was actually happy it was a slow night for business, so I could linger at the taxi stand and bear witness.

I then noticed a lanky boy on my side of the street, crouching at the border of City Hall Park. His eyes and hair were dark black, and he wore baggy green dungarees and a black T-shirt. One of his hands was draped atop a skateboard balanced perpendicularly on its end. The board looked as if it had once been intricately painted, but was now mostly worn down and battered. Clearly, this board had been through the wars. The boy sat in solitude as he quietly watched the activity across the way. Then, suddenly, he rose, dropped the board and skated across the street.

This kid's presence, his effect on his peers, was startling. The other boys noticed him, literally stopped in their tracks and spontaneously gathered at the sidewalk's edge to watch. Skateboarders are cocky; to weave through the cityscape while fending off cars and evading the police requires an almost reckless self-confidence. But this young man appeared serene; his belief in his own ability had transcended beyond the grasp of ego. He made his turn at the Flynn and paused for a moment before pushing off and rolling west.

He rode toward the Vermont House with not a shred of wasted movement, his body the opposite of jerky. It brought to mind an older woman who did Tai Chi every evening at dusk in the Waterfront Park last summer. For a split second, it seemed that everything else was in motion, while he was in perfect stillness. He hit the ramp at gazelle speed, accelerated across the entranceway and was airborne.

I could swear somebody hit the slow motion button. I watched him go into a circle, his eyes smiling, his body graceful and buoyant. It looked like, if he so desired, he could have executed another two or even three turns while he was up there, seemingly suspended in air. He had, it appeared, all the time in the world.

He hit the ground cat-like; beyond a slight flexing at the knees, I detected no signs of the landing's impact. He hopped the curb and continued straight down Main Street, disappearing amidst the glow of the car and street lights.

That's the way it's done, I thought to myself, as the teenager in me bowed his head silently in respect.

The Words of the Poet

The Huntington Apartments, née the Huntington Hotel, is no more. A piece of kitchen equipment in the street-level Bagel Bakery caught fire, and the ensuing blaze caused irreparable damage to the entire edifice.

For Burlingtonians this is not a news flash, having occurred last spring. The primary downtown taxi stand is located across the street from this structure, so I've spent hours gazing at it. The building is undergoing a complete renovation. I would say it's proceeding at a snail's pace (having never met a cliché I didn't like), but that would disparage the comparative blazing speed of some gastropods I've known. Let's just say that, at the current rate of work, the beautiful new apartment complex promised in the artist's rendering will begin renting around the time the Bush twins hit menopause.

In its previous incarnation as the Huntington Apartments, the owners had painted the building a dismal gray green — a color evoking the cozy ambience of Dannemora Prison. As an element of the renovation, two workers have been painstakingly scrubbing off this paint with all manner of chemical sprays, industrial brushes and your basic elbow grease. The gradually emerging brickwork is lovely, with pale granite flecks highlighting the top corners of each window. Early builders had a sense of grace, it seems.

On the lower level, the windows of the closed businesses are boarded over with sheets of plywood. This calls to mind the wall that for many years enclosed the hole in the ground where the venerable Strong Hardware store had stood, before it, too, burned in the huge blaze of 1971. For the longest time, these boards functioned as unofficial, though sanctioned, town billboards. Works of art, political treatises and street poetry mixed together in an odd yet aesthetically pleasing harmony. All things must pass, but I've always missed this communal, largely noncommercial expression of the Queen City psyche.

Almost as soon as the boards went up at the Huntington Apartments site, poetry snippets began to appear, and continued to accrue over the ensuing months. For some reason, it heartened me immensely that these poetic expressions were never subject to defacement or vulgar overwrites — or for that matter, removal.

Cognizant that my delighted reaction to these wall musings might well belong in the maybe-it's-just-me-department, I put it to the test. Strolling downtown with a friend, I enthusiastically pointed out the graffiti as we came upon the building. He took a gander and didn't hesitate.

"Jernigan, I really don't think this stuff is poetry," he said. Our friendship was such that he didn't need to coddle my feelings. "It's totally banal."

This is a guy whose aesthetic sensibility I greatly respect; his comment definitely made me rethink my opinion. But one man's poetry is, well, another man's graffiti. When it comes to art, we're talking subjectivity, and for some reason the Huntington writings intrigued and moved me.

So, trite or profound? You be the judge. But keep in mind the context: big, colored letters on the walls of a burnt-out downtown building.

First appeared, "THINGS R NEVER ALWAYS WHAT THEY SEEM, YA KNOW?" *Wow*, I thought — *ain't that the truth*?

The next one — "U ARE WHAT YOU ARE" — hit me like a Zen koan, running through my mind for two days.

A week later, "BREW ME UP SOME TWINING TEA AND TELL ME THAT U ♥ ME." This little ditty transported me forthwith to the movie *A Room With A View,* romantic sucker that I am.

There were then a couple of pithy eulogies: "PRINCESS DIANA, QUEEN OF HEARTS. MISS YOU" and "CLARINET MAN — MORE THAN MUSIC." Accompanying the good-bye to Richard Haupt — a well-known local street musician, recently departed — was a crude, yet somehow perfect rendering of a clarinet.

"REFEREE WON'T BLOW THE WHISTLE." *A trenchant commentary on life's intrinsic unfairness*, I thought.

The last offering I remember was, "I DON'T WANNA FALL IN LUV — AM I THE ONLY ONE?" That just about says it all for the closing chapter of the 20th century, don't you think?

What a generous outpouring, these writing created by — I don't know — a single individual? A guerilla poetry collective? This was art produced and delivered free-of-charge: unpackaged, unfettered and uncensored. These plywood scribes were not selling anything, they were just sharing their hearts and minds with all of us, simply because it's the most natural thing to do.

I found all of this was very inspiring. The day after John Denver's untimely death, someone took on the one remaining blank board: "ALMOST HEAVEN, WEST VIRGINIA, BLUE RIDGE MOUNTAIN, SHENANDOAH RIVER. THANKS JOHN. R.I.P."

I'm not saying who wrote this, but maybe he went to Boutilier's Art Center and found the perfect bar of thick, orange chalk. Perhaps he thought about John Denver, who, despite his unhip, pretentious public image, created songs that, at their best, evoked the heart-opening grandeur and beauty of the natural world.

Then maybe this writer approached the plywood and experienced a sudden flash of being in grade school, standing before the wide expanse of the blackboard, with nobody else in the classroom. It could be that he wrote out the tribute carefully and deliberately, in his best block penmanship, and then stepped back a moment to contemplate his work. And — I'm purely guessing here — I bet you he felt great.

9

THE WES AND ELLEN TRILOGY

Ever receive a wondrous gift, something you had no idea you even needed before the fact? That's exactly my experience of Wes and Ellen coming into my life. Both individually and as a couple, these two people gave me something I needed, something that fills my life to this day.

Ellen Berman

"My goodness, do you see the moon tonight, Jernigan? It's sitting right on the mountains."

"I sure do, Ellen. It's something, all right."

Above us the night sky was a black slate set off by a piercing gibbous moon under a shower of diamond stars. *God's Christmas display*, I thought to myself. A recent snowfall cloaked the Green Mountains, the fresh white coat glowing in the moonlight like some improbable white lava. It felt cozy in the cab as we sped along the Bolton Flats *en route* to Ellen's Northfield residence. Knowing that just outside our mobile, metal cocoon the temperature shuddered at 10 below only accentuated the taxi's gift of warmth and protection.

"Jernigan, the moon is moving around the sky! It was just on the left side of the car, and now it's on the right. How does it do that?"

I turned and smiled at my customer of 10 years. Ellen Berman is not quite five feet tall, but sturdy, buxom and surprisingly spry for her 86 years. Her blue eyes shone brightly, eagerly awaiting the answer to her question.

"Well, Ellen, the moon isn't really moving. It's just as the road turns and the car shifts, the position of the moon goes from one side of us to the other."

This was by no means a lucid explanation, but in my defense, it was the third time I was delivering the moon lecture in the course of this ride. It's hard to remain articulate repeatedly answering the same, well, inane question. On the other hand, perhaps I should have had it down pat, because Ellen had been asking me about the moon for months now, whenever it's been visible during our nighttime return trips to Northfield. Her dementia has advanced over this year, and her short-term memory is close to nonexistent at this point.

"When will I be visiting Wes again?" Ellen asked, her brow furrowing with hope.

"Next Wednesday, Ellen," I replied, and reached over to give her shoulder a soft squeeze. "Every Wednesday I take you."

"Oh, yes. I asked you that before." She shook her head and sighed. Indeed, she had asked me about our next visit 15 minutes earlier. "I have a mind like a sieve."

I chuckled at that well-worn simile, and said, "That's OK, Ellen. You go ahead and ask me as many times as you like."

On a weekly basis for the past 10 years, I have been driving Ellen to visit with her companion, Wes Epstein, at the Wake Robin senior community in Shelburne. Until a few years ago, the commuting was reciprocal, and I would frequently take Wes to visit Ellen at her apartment in Montpelier, and later at the Mayo Nursing Home when she had to move there. But Wes himself would be turning 90 his next birthday, and was now essentially non-ambulatory; the round-trip between Shelburne and Northfield had become more than his frail body could handle.

As the Stowe exit came and went, I thought about my decade-long relationship with this customer. Since the mid-'90s, I have spent more time with Ellen and Wes than anyone else in my world, with the possible exception of my closest blood relatives. Ellen has pronounced me her "unofficial stepson," and I think she got it just about right. The two of us have hundreds of conversational hours under our belts, and I might know more about Ellen's life than my actual mother's.

I know about her childhood in the slums of the Bronx; about her mother eventually throwing out her abusive father. She's told me how, at age nine, she was sent upstate to a home for orphaned Jewish girls because her mother couldn't afford to adequately care for both her children, and therefore made the "Sophie's Choice" to keep just her son.

I've heard how the orphanage was "the best thing" that ever happened to Ellen, and about the great food, clothes and education she received there, eventually becoming a dental hygienist. I know about her marriage to Phil Berman, a music publicist who introduced many major Country-and-Western artists to New York City. Ellen's told me of the day that Phil, age 39, suffered a major coronary in his office and died on the spot.

I know about how Ellen then suffered a total emotional breakdown and lost custody of her only child, a son they called Chet — with whom she has no contact to this day. I learned how, after two lost years and a move to Florida, she suddenly popped out of her depression and took an office job with the state government. Ellen's told me about retiring and moving to Vermont in the early '90s. And she's told me about the spring day she met the second true love of her life, Wes Epstein, on a tennis court in Montpelier.

The moon was still sneaking around the sky when we arrived back at the Mayo in Northfield. "Hey, Ellen," I said as we eased to a stop at the entrance and I shifted the taxi into park. "Do you know what the moon is made out of?"

"No, I don't, Jernigan. Tell me."

"It's made out of cheddar cheese."

We both laughed heartily, though I've told this "joke" a hundred times. "Jernigan," she said, grasping my forearm, "you are such a kidder!"

Ellen held my arm as we passed through the wide double doors leading into the nursing home. Walking together through the pastel-painted corridor, she asked me, "When will I be moving home, Jernigan?"

I stopped and took both her hands in mine. "Ellen, this is where you live now. It's the Mayo. They take real good care of you here."

"Oh, dear — I have I mind like a sieve. I just can't remember anything."

"Don't worry, Ellen," I said, looking into those misty blue eyes, "I'll remember for you."

Wes Epstein

The idea of talking to Wes had been bubbling in my mind for a few months. The guy, after all, was 89; if there was something I needed to get off my chest, this was a classic case of "time's a-wasting."

I was driving along Route 7, on my way to his place at the Wake Robin senior community in Shelburne. This was a regular fare that had begun in the mid-'90s: facilitating the weekly visits between Wes and his companion, Ellen Berman, who used to have an apartment in Montpelier but now resided at the Mayo Nursing Home in Northfield. In the early years, Wes would often be the commuter, but now that he was confined to bed or a wheelchair, Ellen was the one who made the round-trips.

It was a quarter to seven on a mild evening, approaching the time I was scheduled to pick up Ellen for her return trip to Northfield. As I traversed the road-widening construction zone, now safely buttoned up for the winter, my mind drifted to my first meeting with Wes.

It was some 10 years ago when he happened to catch my cab at the Burlington bus terminal. His hair back then was already silky white and, though he walked with a cane and a slightly stooped posture, he projected an air of strength and vigor. I recall him sitting in the front with me, and that we got into a conversation about, of all things, alternative medicine.

And here's the thing about that first conversation, something that has held true as the years have gone by: We were entirely simpatico, not just in our views on the subject, but in our personalities. In our goofy optimism, we were two of a kind — kindred spirits.

I pulled into the neat little community of Wake Robin, a village unto itself. By any measure, it's an attractive development offering all manner of amenities and services. Although the residents are a wealthy bunch — the costs of getting in excludes all but the top economic tier of retirees — my experience reveals anything but a population of buttoned-down, snobbish types. This community, by design or chance, attracts artists, teachers, free-thinkers — a group into which Wes had effortlessly fit.

Because he was a humble man, it took me years to discover just how illustrious a life Wes had led. For starters, he was a resident Rhodes scholar at Oxford in prewar England, becoming a key part of the team that developed penicillin. After the war, he was named physician representative to the United Nations relief mission to Byelorussia, a Russian province that had been utterly devastated and occupied during the German advance on Moscow. Back in the states in the late '40s, Wes's history of progressive political advocacy ran headlong into the Cold War and Red Scare. He refused to "name names," and was essentially forced to resign his post with the U.S. Public Health Service.

Though his separation from government work was a challenge to a man with a young family to support, he soon found work with the United Mine Workers. For the next 20 years he lived in Pittsburgh doing pioneering work as a medical administrator for the union. In the '60s he became deeply involved in the civil-rights movement, and he topped off his professional career as president of a black medical college in Nashville.

Of course, when Wes came into my life, he was long since retired. My experience was strictly of the man, not his worldly accomplishments. And through the years, he has taught me, not by words, but by living example. He's modeled for me a way to treat people with kindness and affection; he's showed me how to age with dignity and grace, never voicing a shred of self-pity or regret, even as his basic physical functioning — dressing himself, walking, reading — faded away like old paint.

I parked at the Skilled Nursing Unit, said hello to a couple of staff people at the main desk, and walked up to Wes's room. I knocked a few times, and waited before entering. Despite their status as octogenarians, Wes and Ellen had a little of the teenager in them, and I was always careful lest I interrupt a moment of intimacy.

"Hellooo," came the bass voice of Wes from inside the room. "Jernigan, is that you?"

"It sure is," I replied, letting myself in. Wes was sitting in his easy chair. He said, "Ellen's in the ladies room."

I sat down on the bed facing him, and he smiled at me warmly. "Wes," I said, "there's something I been meaning to tell you."

"OK," he replied, and nodded at me, his blue eyes open and inviting on his long, lined face.

"Wes, what I want to tell you is, the way you've treated me through the years has really made a difference to my life. I mean, the way you listen to me, and take an interest in the things I do. I'd never really gotten that kind of caring from an older man and, well . . ."

I was crying now, tears rolling down my face, over my lips into my mouth. Wes just kept looking at me intently.

"What I'm trying to say," I rallied, "is that you've been like a father to me, and for all that and more I want to thank you."

Wes brought his hand to his heart but didn't say a word. He just smiled and nodded. Ellen came out of the bathroom, walked over and put an arm around Wes's shoulder. She said, "Now what have you boys been talking about?"

"Oh, nothing special," Wes replied, and turned to give me wink. "You know, Ellen — just about this and that."

Wes & Ellen

Ellen Berman said little as we drove along Highway 89 on a bleak Sunday afternoon. We were heading to Wake Robin, the senior living community in Shelburne that has been the home of Wes Epstein, Ellen's companion of the last decade.

For nearly as long as these two had been a couple, I have been the transportation link making their visits possible. Gradually, as the weeks turned into months and then years, I had slipped beyond the role of cabdriver into that of adoptive stepson. This had occurred naturally; the two of them were warm, affectionate people, and I couldn't help but reciprocate.

When I think about how cruel this world can be, I feel like the presence of love is a miracle in its every manifestation. On one level, all romantic unions are the same whatever the age of the couple. It's all about two people connecting and finding something in each other which propels them into a higher experience of life. But, on another level, each stage of love is specific: in the lessons to be had, and in the beauty and nobility that is imparted.

In witnessing Wes and Ellen's relationship, I'd had the opportunity to learn about a kind of love I'd not before experienced. These two souls had found one another in their final phase of life, and they loved each other with a purity of heart perhaps only possible in this poignant late chapter — when there's nothing to prove, no place to go, no goals to achieve.

About a half-hour earlier, I'd picked up Ellen at the Mayo Nursing Home in Northfield. As we settled into my taxi, she had been her usual chipper self, which only made what I had to tell her that much more excruciating. But there was no beating around the bush, and no way to soften the blow.

"Ellen," I said, turning in my seat and taking her hands in mine. "There's something really sad I have to tell you. Wes had a major heart attack this week, and the tests show there's nothing they can do to help. They're saying he doesn't have long to live."

"Noooo!" Ellen cried out, and began sobbing intensely, her entire body expressing the devastating shock of the reality I had just delivered. "No, it can't be," she continued. "He should be at the hospital where the doctors can do something to help him."

"Oh, Ellen, that's the thing. His heart was so badly damaged, and he's 89 years old. There's nothing medical to be done. That's why they transferred him back to Wake Robin, so he can rest comfortably and have all his family around."

"No, no — it can't be. The doctors *have* to help him. He should be back at the hospital." She began sobbing again. I embraced her and we cried together for about a minute, and then we got underway.

Now, as we rolled down the highway, every so often Ellen would ask, in the most forlorn voice, "Did you say that Wes had a heart attack?" I couldn't tell if this was the dementia — her short-term memory was just about shot — or the natural defense mechanism of denial. In any event, each time she asked I would again recount the painful string of events, and she would begin crying anew. I kept my right arm around her as I drove, trying to comfort her as much as I could. Or perhaps, we were comforting each other.

When we arrived at the Skilled Nursing Unit at Wake Robin, I asked Ellen to wait in the car and I went in. A staff person at the main desk intercepted me as I walked past — not a good sign. She looked stricken.

"Jernigan," she said softly. "Could you please wait here for a moment. I'm going to get a family member from Wes's room."

I don't remember the next two minutes. I knew what was coming and my mind went blank, my emotions numb. One of Wes's four children, a son, came out to me and said, "Wes passed away 15 minutes ago. It was incredibly peaceful, Jernigan. He was barely breathing one minute, and then we noticed he had stopped."

"Oh, I'm so sorry," I said. "What about Ellen? Should we bring her in?"

"Why don't you ask her?" he replied.

I walked with Ellen into Wes's room. His son was quietly shuffling through some papers on a desk, and Wes's elder daughter was sitting at the foot of the bed. Wes was lying there covered by a white sheet, his head and shoulders exposed. He did, indeed, look peaceful.

Ellen rushed to his bedside, almost falling. "Oh, Wes," she said, grasping his arm. "He's warm," she said to the three other living souls in the room. "Maybe he's just sleeping."

"I'm sorry, Ellen," I said. "He's still warm because he just passed away." She then began sobbing, and I went over to steady her. The room had a holy feeling. The only experience I can compare it to is a birth I once attended.

Wes's daughter stood up and walked passed the window. I noticed it was open about 10 inches on this typical Vermont winter afternoon. She looked at me, and her face was immeasurably sad, yet also peaceful like her dad's.

"I opened the window," she said. "In case Wes's soul had to fly away to wherever his journey is taking him."

For additional copies of this book or
Hackie: Cab Driving and Life,
visit your favorite bookstore or order online
at the official *Hackie* website:

www.yohackie.com